The Rent-a-Wife Agency Can Help With _All_ Your Household Needs....

Need somebody to do the cooking? The cleaning? All those tiresome tasks you've got no time for in your busy schedule? (And, being a man, wouldn't know how to do right, anyway?) No problem! Why, after just a day or two with your new Rent-a-Wife around the house, you'll wonder how you ever got along _without_ her!

And yes—although it _is_ a rather unusual request—she'll even pretend she's your real bride-to-be. (No, no, you don't have to explain why you want to convince your mother you're getting married.) In fact, your Rent-a-Wife will be so convincing, _you_ may just start thinking she's the real thing—or _wanting_ her to be....

Dear Reader,

Have you ever had a time when you wished you could be two people at once? You know, so one of you could lead your regular life and the other one could see those same people incognito to find out what they were really like (and what they really thought of you)? In Alexandra Sellers' *Occupation: Millionaire*, heroine Tallia Venables pretty much gets that chance. One of her is gorgeous, the other a bit of a plain Jane. The big surprise is what she finds out about sexy Brad Slinger in the process! You're really going to enjoy this one.

And don't miss Kelly Jamison's *The Bride Was a Rental*. Sam Weller is a confirmed bachelor, but suddenly he needs a phony fiancée—fast! Enter Ginger Marsh, willing to take the job but not quite what Sam had in mind. She's a whole lot more than he expected, not to mention a whole lot…sexier. Playing house has never been this much fun before!

Have a good time with both of this month's books, and don't forget to come back next month for two more delightful tales all about meeting—not to mention marrying!—Mr. Right.

Yours,

Leslie Wainger
Senior Editor and Editorial Coordinator

Please address questions and book requests to:
Silhouette Reader Service
U.S.: 3010 Walden Ave., P.O. Box 1325, Buffalo, NY 14269
Canadian: P.O. Box 609, Fort Erie, Ont. L2A 5X3

KELLY JAMISON

The Bride Was a Rental

SILHOUETTE YOURS TRULY™

Published by Silhouette Books

America's Publisher of Contemporary Romance

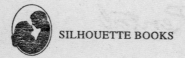

SILHOUETTE BOOKS

ISBN 0-373-52066-2

THE BRIDE WAS A RENTAL

Printed in U.S.A.

A Note From Kelly Jamison

I was rummaging in the refrigerator for chocolate one day when something (temporary insanity?) made me take stock of the house. Dirty dishes lay in the sink, an anemic-looking chicken sat in the freezer waiting for a gourmet touch, laundry reached to the ceiling, and the weeds choked my flower beds. I said to myself, "I need a wife." Since I'm a happily married woman, another wife in the house was out of the question from my standpoint. But the idea got me to thinking about how much easier life would be if a person could just rent a wife. Let's face it—despite sexual equality, wives are the ones usually stuck with the less-than-appealing household chores. And then I thought, *What if a confirmed bachelor was desperate enough to rent a wife? What if his mother was coming to visit, and she had a plan to get him married? What if…?*

And that's how *The Bride Was a Rental* took shape. Hundreds of chocolate bars and dirty dishes later, I hope you have as much fun reading it as I had writing it. And let me know what you do about those dust balls the size of dump trucks hiding behind the refrigerator. Write to: Kelly Jamison, P.O. Box 5223, Quincy, Illinois, 62305.

Books by Kelly Jamison

Silhouette Yours Truly

The Bride Was a Rental

Silhouette Desire

Echoes from the Heart #579
Hearts in Hiding #626
Heartless #760
Will #798
The Daddy Factor #885
Forsaken Father #930
Unexpected Father #1092

Silhouette Special Edition

The Wedding Contract #1014

1

My Dear Son,

By now you may have forgotten what I said when I came to see you last year, or you may have thought that I wasn't serious. I was definitely serious, Sam. I gave you one year to find a wife. I'm coming back, and since you are no closer to being married this year than you were last year, I'm taking matters into my own hands. Much as I love Hawaii, I intend to stay in Missouri with you until I have found you a wife. I will arrive on Monday at the St. Louis airport. I've sent your sister the arrival time and flight number, so she can pick me up. And don't bother trying to call me to talk me out of it. I won't answer the phone. See you on Monday.

Aloha,
Mother

Sam Weller cursed so loudly that the beagle lying just inside the front door pricked up his ears and briefly glanced at the couch, as if considering whether this was a good time to hide under it. But Sam strode past him and on into the kitchen, where he slammed the rest of the mail onto the table. Ratso the beagle sighed and rolled over onto his side. He opened one eye a moment later, when Sam came back from the kitchen, the letter in his hand, grabbed his cowboy hat from the doorknob and pushed open the screen door on his way out. The pickup truck started, then left so quickly that gravel sprayed the front step.

Ratso closed his eyes and went back to sleep.

When the pickup pulled into their driveway in town, Pete Candelini looked at his wife, Jeannie, who was on the phone.

"Got to go, Mother," she said in a lowered voice. "Here he comes now. Your letter must have just arrived, right on schedule."

"Are you sure this is a good idea?" Pete asked when she hung up.

"It's inspired," Jeannie assured him, getting up to open the door. "Sam just needs a push."

"Have you heard about this?!" Sam demanded without prelude, bounding up the walk and into the house as he pushed his hat back on his head. "Monday! She's arriving *Monday!* And this is Saturday!"

Pete wondered again if this was a good idea. Sam looked more like a man who'd been punched than one who'd been given a little push.

Jeannie nodded sympathetically and kissed her brother on the cheek, stretching up on tiptoe to reach him.

"Why did she have to pick on me?" Sam asked Pete. He was pacing the tiny kitchen like a tiger in a cage.

"She did warn you last year," Pete said. "You've had twelve months to think of some way out of this."

Sam gnashed his teeth.

"I didn't take her seriously until I got that letter. We have got to do something. I can't survive having Mother trying to matchmake for me."

"She *is* determined to find you a wife this time," Jeannie said innocently. "And you know how she is when her mind is made up."

"She won't go home until she thinks she's done her job," Pete concurred.

"I'm doomed," Sam said, sitting down in a chair, misery etched on his face. He drummed his fingers on the table, then absently plucked up a chocolate chip cookie and popped it into his mouth. His brows knit together as he sat thinking.

Jeannie exchanged another look with Pete.

"It's a shame we can't pull one over on Mother for once," Jeannie ventured, one eye on Sam.

He gave a noncommittal grunt and ate another cookie.

"If we could get someone to play the part, this would really set Mother back on her ear," she continued. "And save your precious bachelorhood," she added, almost as an afterthought.

"Play what part?" Sam asked, glancing up at her with a frown.

Jeannie smiled. "Get someone to be your fiancée, just until Mother goes back home satisfied that you're on your way to the altar." Her smile widened. "It would serve her right, after all her meddling."

"Where are we going to find someone to pretend to be my fiancée on such short notice?" Sam asked, shaking his head.

"Well…we could try Rent-a-Wife." Jeannie sat back, waiting for his reaction.

"Pardon me?" he asked.

"It's a new business in town, Rent-a-Wife. You remember me telling you about it. Ginger Marsh owns it. She moved here from St. Louis a couple of months ago."

Sam scowled. "Not the woman you've been trying to set me up with for the last month."

"But this is different," Jeannie protested. "This wouldn't be actually dating her. You'd pay her for her time."

"And she'd pretend to be my fiancée?" Sam asked. "Sorry, Jeannie. It's as harebrained as one of Mother's schemes."

"And what better way to turn the tables on her?" Jeannie said, grinning.

Sam sat thinking, staring off into space, and Jeannie kicked Pete under the table when he started to say something.

"I guess it's a better idea than any I've come up with," Sam said finally. "But what if this Ginger Marsh woman won't do it?"

"She will," Jeannie assured him. "She needs the money."

Sam's eyebrows went up again.

"She's a widow just getting her business off the ground, and she could use more customers," Jeannie assured him. "Last week when I had to work overtime, I hired her to do a week's worth of dinners for us. She's a wonderful cook." Jeannie looked at him pointedly. "She baked those cookies."

Sam stopped with the cookie halfway to his mouth, inspecting it as if he suspected it had a hook hidden somewhere inside. He frowned at Jeannie again.

"I get it," he said slowly.

"Get what?" Jeannie said innocently, recognizing that look on her brother's face.

"I get what you're up to, little sister," Sam growled. "Just because I turned down that date you set up with this Marsh woman, you and Mother cooked up this half-baked idea to force me to go out with her. You're a conniving woman, Jeannie Candelini, and I'm not falling for your little ploy."

"All right," Jeannie said blithely. "Then you'll have to face the consequences."

"What consequences?"

Jeannie held up a piece of paper. "Mother's flight schedule. She's coming whether you call Ginger or not. And yes, I admit that I like Ginger and I'd like you to get to know her. And it would do you good to do some dating for a change. But if you're determined to suffer through the blind dates from hell that Mother will drag out to the ranch, then that's your business."

Sam grimaced. He knew when to retreat.

Holding his hands in the air, he said, "All right, General. I'll accept your terms."

"You've made the right decision," Jeannie assured him as she pushed him toward the door. "You go on home. I'll call Ginger and ask her to stop by your place for an interview. You can make up your mind then."

"This is only temporary," Sam told her firmly. "No woman is getting me to the altar again, and you can bet good money on that. So don't think your little plan will lead to anything permanent."

"Understood," Jeannie said with an angelic smile, her eyes sparkling.

Ginger Marsh pulled her car to the side of the road and consulted the hand-drawn map again. "This looks like the right turn,'' she said to the little girl beside her. ''It should be somewhere just up ahead.''

''Wow, we're out in the middle of nowhere,'' her daughter marveled, swiveling her head to look at the cornfields on either side.

''Not quite, Emily,'' Ginger said. ''But we're definitely approaching the exit ramp to the middle of nowhere.''

Emily giggled, and Ginger smiled at her as she pulled back onto the road. All Jeannie Candelini had told Ginger when she called an hour ago was that her brother needed some help cleaning up his house and he might evolve into a steady client. Jeannie had asked that she go see Sam Weller right that minute, if possible, and when Ginger asked why the hurry, Jeannie had said, ''I think there's a storm coming.''

The sky looked perfectly blue, Ginger thought as she drove on, bluer than she remembered it being in St. Louis, where she and Emily had lived before the move to little London, Missouri, on the Mississippi River. She was enjoying the slower pace of life in a small town, a place where the weather was as important a topic as how the corn and soybean markets were doing.

It was a little scary, but exciting as well, to be on her own. She was looking forward to busy days and quiet evenings uninterrupted by phone calls from testosterone-driven males with their promises of brightening the lonely widow's day—and night. Ginger was more interested in peace and quiet than a social life.

She loved Saturdays like this, when she and Emily could go for a drive and browse in antique stores or get an ice cream cone at a small soda counter.

''What do you say we have ourselves a picnic when

we get back home?'' Ginger suggested. "We could go down by the river and watch the towboats.''

"Neat!'' Emily concurred. Her wavy red hair was escaping the clasp at the back, and Ginger brushed it back fondly. Emily's enthusiasm for everything had been a joy since they moved. Ginger didn't know what she would have done if Emily hated the town. But seven-year-old Emily had considered the whole move a big adventure.

"It should be around here somewhere,'' Ginger said, consulting the map again.

Ginger braked when she rounded a curve and found herself at the entrance to the ranch. Sam Weller Purebred Angus read the wooden sign mounted over the drive. Fields stretched away on both sides, and Ginger could see black cattle everywhere.

She pulled into the gravel driveway slowly, unable to stop looking at the fields and the cattle grazing in the sun. It was a warm, lush, lazy September morning, the kind she had never really appreciated when she lived in the city. Here it seemed as if the sky stretched out like an ocean, and even the trees were greener than in the city.

"Welcome to 'Bonanza,'" Ginger murmured with a low whistle.

She stopped the car in front of the white frame house, too focused on the impending interview to notice much beyond the black shutters and wooden steps. Taking a deep breath, she went up to the screen door, Emily trailing behind her. The wooden door was open, so obviously he was home, or else he was less than concerned about burglars.

Ginger rapped sharply on the screen door. A fly droned above her head.

"Mr. Weller?" she called, shading her eyes to try to see into the house.

"I'm right here."

Both Ginger and Emily jumped and turned around at the sound of his voice behind them. He was standing at the foot of the steps, wiping his hands on a bandanna that he shoved into his jeans pocket. He wore blue jeans, dirty and torn, but still formfitting, and Ginger tried not to look at the long expanse of hard thigh they outlined. His once-white T-shirt was also smudged and torn. He wore a black cowboy hat that effectively concealed his eyes, but Ginger saw the wary tension in his strong jaw. She began to wonder just what Jeannie Candelini had gotten her into when she strongly suggested that Ginger visit Sam Weller.

He abruptly pushed the hat back, and Ginger stared into his eyes. They were a steely blue, and sharply appraising. A shock of blond hair fell across his forehead, and he pushed it back impatiently.

"Mr. Weller," she said politely, "I'm Ginger Marsh, and this is my daughter Emily." She waited, but he didn't say anything, just studied her with those incredible eyes. She was growing uncomfortable and a little irritated as his eyes roved slowly lower in an obvious and arrogant inspection. "I believe your sister told you about me," she prompted him sharply.

Jeannie had left out several pertinent facts, Sam thought as he looked at Ginger Marsh. One, she was pretty. Two, she had a daughter. And three, she was *damn* pretty. He had paid scant attention when Jeannie tried to set him up on a date with Ginger Marsh a few weeks ago, and he had barely listened when she gave him the vital information on her earlier today. Now he tried to recall the particulars. Jeannie had said that she was a widow and that she had moved here a couple of months ago.

Ginger was feeling more uncomfortable by the moment. Sam Weller was obviously the tall, silent type. And he was tall. Even from her position four steps above him, he looked intimidating.

"Jeannie said you might want to hire me for some work around your house," she said hesitantly. "You do have a sister named Jeannie Candelini, don't you, Mr. Weller?" she asked at last, with a raise of her eyebrows.

"I do indeed, Mrs. Marsh," he assured her, coming up the steps and shaking her hand. His big hand swallowed hers, and she found herself staring straight ahead at a rock-hard chest. "Please come inside, and we'll see what you think of Jeannie's latest brainstorm."

The way he said "brainstorm" set off a warning in Ginger's head. This wasn't turning out to be the simple job interview she had expected. For one thing, this man was far more attractive than she had expected. And the way he looked her up and down had detonated little frissons of heat all over her skin, even as it annoyed her.

For his part, Sam was trying not to stare at Ginger. He considered the concept of renting a fiancée comparable to the renting of a car. He wanted something solid, dependable and quiet. Not that this woman was flashy. Quite the contrary. But she was like one of those little foreign cars with a luggage rack on the trunk—too cute. In her pink pullover sweater and white jeans, and with that mane of strawberry-blond hair, he couldn't imagine her pushing a heavy vacuum cleaner or standing over a hot stove. She should be lying on a beach somewhere, reading a fashion magazine and sip-ping some sweet lady's drink. He had wanted a Jeep, and here was a Ferrari.

Sam held the screen door for them, and Ginger stepped inside, nearly tripping over something in front of the door. She caught herself and stepped around the white-black-and-brown lump, which groaned. On second look, she could see that the lump was a dog that looked to be part beagle and part slug.

"That's Ratso," Sam said. "He's five years old, and he's energy-challenged."

Ginger glanced back and caught Sam Weller eyeing her backside. He looked away immediately, and she flushed.

The house was cool and silent. Ginger saw that the furniture was expensive and tasteful, but obviously hadn't been well cleaned in a long time. It was a modern style that didn't seem to suit the house. Papers were scattered everywhere, and empty plates and coffee mugs sat on the glass coffee table and the carpeted floor.

Jeannie had told her that Sam Weller was divorced, but somehow Ginger had expected to find more traces of the woman who had once been his wife. But there was nothing other than the furniture, which Ginger was sure that the wife and not Sam had chosen.

The kitchen was large, and devoid of any feminine touches, as well. No curtains at the windows. No notes or magnets on the refrigerator. The counters were bare, only a frayed dishrag lying draped over the edge of the sink.

Sam brought them to the corner of the room and seated them at a battered rectangular oak table covered with newspapers and scraps of paper. The chairs were oak, as well, and plain.

The ex–Mrs. Sam Weller must have gone off with the modern set here, Ginger thought. But this table suited the house more than the rest of the furniture did.

"We have beer, milk, and more beer," he said over the top of the refrigerator door.

"Thank you, but we really don't need anything," Ginger said.

"Yes, you do," Sam said pointedly.

"Milk then, please."

"You'll be sorry you didn't take the beer," he warned her as he put three glasses on the table and poured milk from a plastic carton. "Once the discussion gets going," he added with a raise of his brows. He took off his hat and dropped it on the remaining empty chair. He was tanned from a summer of working outside, and his blue eyes nearly blazed in that bronze face.

Ginger took a long sip of milk to fortify herself.

"What kind of discussion?" she asked warily.

"A discussion about my…problem," he said, leaning forward on his forearms and meeting her eyes.

Ginger cleared her throat hesitantly. "Emily," she said, "maybe you would like to take your milk outside and look for butterflies." Ginger directed her gaze back to Sam. "Providing there aren't any dangerous… *varmints* lurking around."

Sam smiled wryly at her choice of words. He was almost sure she had him categorized as one of those alleged varmints, at this point.

"Perfectly safe," he assured her. He drained his glass of milk in four large swallows, wondering how to phrase his strange request.

"Now, what is going on here, Mr. Weller?" Ginger asked once the door closed behind Emily.

"My mother, Mrs. Marsh," he said, getting up to put his empty glass in the sink, mostly to put some distance between them, so that he wouldn't be distracted by her big green eyes, now watching him so carefully. He found himself wondering whether that slight pink flush on her cheeks was cosmetics or natural.

"I don't think I'm qualified to solve that kind of problem," Ginger said hesitantly.

"Here's the thing," Sam said, sitting down again, but this time turning the chair around and straddling it, with his arms crossed on the back. "My mother will arrive Monday. If I don't have some pretty good prospects for marriage, she's going to commence matchmaking. And we don't want that, Mrs. Marsh."

"We don't?" she repeated, frowning. Who was this *we*? She wasn't about to be dragged into the middle of some squabble between this man and his mother.

"Definitely not," he assured her. "Now, this next part is tricky." He leaned back slightly and cleared his throat.

Ginger was having a hard time concentrating on what he was saying because of the way his eyes held hers.

"Mrs. Marsh," he said slowly, "I need a fiancée."

Ginger waited, but he didn't go on.

"And?" she prompted him.

"I want to hire you for the job."

"The job?" She still didn't understand what it was he wanted.

"The job as my fiancée, Mrs. Marsh. I want you to help me get this place presentable for Mother's visit, then pose as my fiancée while she's here."

She stared at him blankly for a moment, then said, "You were right. I should have had the beer."

2

"Let me show you the house while I explain," Sam told her, and she followed him numbly. She had no idea what he was up to, but he certainly seemed serious enough. Emily had come back into the house as Sam finished his strange proposal, and now she kept whispering to her mother as she hurried beside her, asking what a fiancée was. Ginger shook her head quickly, and Emily quieted, sighing in frustration.

He gave them a tour, explaining absolutely nothing about his precipitate proposal. Ginger trailed after him through the downstairs, inspecting the living room, dining room and family room, all of which were filled with dusty, sterile-looking furniture.

There were three bedrooms upstairs, and two full baths, each of them a disaster area. One of the bedrooms was apparently used for storage. Boxes and a mattress were piled against the wall.

The bed and dresser in the room where Ginger assumed Sam slept were nice enough, but they were piled high with papers and books and assorted knickknacks. The bed was unmade and had no spread, only a thin, worn blanket in an ugly shade of brown. Ginger grimaced, and Sam caught the slight movement.

"You see what I'm up against here?" he asked dryly.

"Not exactly," she said as she followed him back downstairs. "If it's housecleaning you want, that's simple enough. Why do you want a fiancée?" And why didn't this good-looking male specimen already have a bevy of girlfriends lining up to clean his house and cook his meals? Every time she looked into his eyes, she could feel heat rushing to every sensitive spot in her body.

"I want to *appear* to have a fiancée," he said, showing them to the kitchen table again.

Ratso, who had barely opened one eye when they came through on the tour, now began snoring.

Ginger sat down slowly, still confused. "Why?"

"My mother," Sam said ominously. "She descends on my house once a year, fusses over everything and encourages me to find a wife. Mission failed, she goes home to Hawaii again. But this year is different."

"How so?" she asked, intrigued in spite of herself.

"Last year she told me that if I wasn't married or engaged by her visit this year, she was staying until I put a ring on some woman's finger."

Ginger couldn't help the smile that twitched the corners of her mouth.

"You think this is funny," he said accusingly. "But you haven't met my mother."

"Mr. Weller, may I ask you a question?" she said, still unsuccessful at hiding her smile. "How old are you?"

He tightened his jaw. "I know, I know. I'll be forty years old in December, and you think I'm too old to let my mother interfere in my life. Well, you're wrong. Just ask Jeannie. Jeannie and Pete were going to live together, and maybe get married in a couple of years. Mother got wind of that and got into town faster than a meteor. She dragged three ministers with her, as well as a Hare Krishna who'd been passing out literature at the airport. Then she set about organizing the wedding. One minister baked the cake, the second addressed the invitations, and the third altered the wedding dress. And the Hare Krishna grew his hair out and played the wedding march on a guitar.''

"I think you're exaggerating," Ginger said, rolling her eyes.

"Only slightly. Mrs. Marsh, I like peace and quiet. I like to run my own life. And I like solitude. I will have none of those things until my mother is satisfied that I'm on my way down the aisle to the altar.''

"But, pretending to be engaged..." she said, shaking her head despite her amusement. "Your mother will see right through your charade."

Sam shook his head. "She's too intent on getting what she wants. Pete and Jeannie will cooperate, and hardly anyone else has to know. Believe me, I want Mother leaving here convinced that I have found a wife, and I fully intend to do that.''

"It still seems like a mean trick to play on her," Ginger said.

"Did I mention that she's now sending Jeannie fertility statues and herbs in hopes of her getting pregnant?"

"You're still exaggerating, right?"

"No, ma'am," he said solemnly.

Ginger sighed. "And once your mother leaves, Emily and I would go back to our normal lives?"

"Mrs. Marsh, I guarantee you I have no desire to date, marry, or otherwise engage the opposite sex in anything other than an occasional conversation." That wasn't entirely true at the moment, however. He was finding it difficult to keep his mind from conjuring up images of what this woman would look like lying on some cool, clean sheets, smiling at her lover. "So don't go getting any ideas," he said, frowning.

Ginger raised her hands, palms out. "Listen, cowboy, I have no intention of doing anything other than what I'm paid to do." She felt herself flushing as she realized how compromising that sounded. "Are you sure your mother won't stay long?" she asked to cover her embarrassment.

"Positive," he guaranteed. "Once she meets my *fiancée* she'll be satisfied and go home after her usual two weeks. And I'll give you a good hourly rate...for *what you're paid to do.*" Ginger flushed again at his reference to her own words. He pulled a slip of paper from his pocket and handed it to her. "What do you say, Mrs. Marsh? All I want are your evenings and weekends until Mother vacates my property. Surely you can handle a little challenge like that."

Ginger swallowed hard at the hourly rate he'd written on the paper. She could certainly use the extra money, especially since she was still getting her business off the ground.

"I have to ask one more thing," she said hesitantly. "As you said, you're almost forty years old. But you've never...remarried?"

He didn't answer for a moment.

"I'm not eager to make that mistake again," he said, his eyes cooling perceptibly. "A ranch like this is no place for a woman, and I like my solitude, Mrs. Marsh. I like it just fine." He gave her a tight smile. "And when Mother's gone, I'll have it back again. If you'll cooperate.'' There was that arrogant tone again that she'd heard him use when he talked about women. Ginger forced herself to remain calm. This was a job, after all. She could put up with a little chauvinism for the money he was going to pay her.

For his part, Sam tried not to think about his doubts. Would his mother ever believe that this attractive woman wanted to live on a ranch?

''You know, your mother's not going to believe you're engaged for one minute if you keep calling me Mrs. Marsh,'' she said at last, wondering whether she was setting a perfectly awful example for Emily by pretending to be this man's fiancée just to fool his mother.

''You'll do it then?'' he asked. ''Ginger,'' he added.

''I'd have to bring Emily with me,'' she warned him.

Sam shrugged. ''Mother loves kids. Emily will be a bonus.''

They both looked at Emily then, and Ginger noted her totally baffled face.

''*What's* going on here?'' Emily demanded.

''We're going to help Sam with his mother's visit,'' Ginger said. ''You and I, my dear, are going to clean this house for him and get some groceries.''

Emily's eyes widened. ''We are? You mean I can help?''

''You got it, kiddo,'' Ginger said. ''I'm going to violate child labor laws here.'' She wiggled her brows at Emily, and Emily laughed.

''Am I a *fee-nancy* too?'' she asked.

Ginger took a deep breath and brushed back the child's hair. ''It's fiancée, honey. It means that a woman has made a promise to a man.'' She glanced at Sam and found her skin tingling again.

"What kind of promise?"

"A serious promise. She promises to take care of that man. She promises to be his best friend." Ginger's eyes raised to Sam's, and he felt a sudden rush of heat to his groin. He had an urge to brush back her hair, the way she had for Emily. He banished the wayward thought the next instant. This was a business agreement between Ginger and him, nothing more. This talk of best friends and taking care of someone sounded nice, but the reality was never quite that pleasant.

"Your father and I made that kind of promise to each other," Ginger went on, her eyes darting away from Sam's face. "I was his fiancée, and then we got married."

"Are you and Mr. Weller going to get married?" Emily asked, her brow knitting.

Ginger took another deep breath. Here came the tough part. She had never lied to Emily, but at the same time, she didn't like the idea of drawing her child into this charade as an active participant.

"Sometimes a man and a woman need time to think about the idea before they get married. Sort of a..." She searched for the right word. "A taste," she concluded. "You remember how the lady at the ice cream shop lets you have a taste of a new flavor before you decide if it's what you want?"

Emily nodded.

"I'm going to be Sam's fiancée, so we can decide if we want to be married. And, in the meantime, we'll be best friends."

She hadn't exactly lied to her child, Ginger told herself. She'd been working so hard to build her business that she had no time to make any close friends here in town. So, in a way, Sam was her best friend, especially considering the time they would be spending together.

"And one other thing, Emily," she said. "If Sam's mother asks you any questions about Sam and me, just tell her you aren't sure. And then let me handle it."

"Okay," Emily said happily. "This is going to be fun."

That wasn't exactly the word Ginger had in mind, but she would honor her part of the agreement.

"So," Ginger said, standing purposefully, "I probably should start cleaning, if your mother's due on Monday."

Sam nodded. "I appreciate it. There's one other point."

"What's that?" Ginger was beginning to think that this man had more strange points than Madonna's underwear.

Sam stood, looking uncomfortable, and shoved his hands in his pockets.

"I need to get you an engagement ring."

"Oh."

Sam saw the surprise cross her face, followed quickly by what could have passed as sadness. Obviously, the suggestion of a ring had brought back some memory of her late husband. But Sam's mother would never believe an engagement that didn't include a ring on the future bride's hand.

"I'm sorry. I didn't mean to make you uncomfortable. But it's something we need to do."

Ginger sighed. He was right.

"If you can wait a moment, I'll go change clothes," he said, "and we can go into town."

"You mean to *buy* an engagement ring?" she said, sounding incredulous. "But that's so expensive."

"Not unless I keep it," he said. "The jeweler is an old friend of mine. We'll find something that's returnable."

She didn't look as reassured as he'd hoped, but she wasn't bolting for the door, either. He left her and Emily in the kitchen while he went upstairs to change clothes.

He could pull this off. He was sure of it. He could pretend that he loved a woman, that he wanted to spend the rest of his life with her. And then he would be alone again. And when his mother called and asked about his fiancée, he would come up with one reason or another why they were postponing the wedding. Once Pete and Jeannie had a baby, his mother would leave him alone, anyway.

A baby. He had thought about it often when he was married. But his wife had wanted to travel, and a baby would have interfered with that. She'd kept putting him off until one day he realized she never intended to have a child.

Well, he had gotten used to that. In fact, he was so used to it that he no longer even thought about babies. Hell, he was too old now, anyway. And he was happy being by himself, working his ranch. He had everything he needed. He shuddered to think of what plans his mother would hatch if she found out that he wasn't really engaged to Ginger. But she wasn't going to find out.

He almost chuckled when he thought of the woman waiting for him downstairs. He had certainly thrown her for a loop with his proposal. But she had recovered. She was just the kind of woman his mother would love. That is, if she bought this whole engagement setup. He'd have to say something to Ginger about her looks.

He didn't like to be critical, but he *was* paying her, and he expected her to look like a potential wife, not a...

A Ferrari in denim.

So why did he have this nagging feeling in the back of his head that he was asking for trouble?

There were browsers in the jewelry shop late Saturday morning, and Sam and Ginger waited until the shop was empty before they approached the counter. They had dropped off Emily at Gladys Turner's house to play with her granddaughter. Gladys owned the fudge shop next door to Ginger's own business.

Sam had looked at the front of Ginger's brick building with interest when they passed it. It had a warm, comfortable feel, from the eyelet curtains at the big front window to the dried flower wreath on the door to the Rent-a-Wife printed in white letters on the green awning.

"Sam!" the older woman behind the counter in the jewelry store called in greeting, smiling as she hustled over to the section of counter where he stood with Ginger. She reached across to ruffle his hair, grinning when he actually blushed.

"Mary Stafford, I've come to warn you," he said, pretending to be stern.

"Warned, now," Mary said, clucking her tongue. "The only event I can imagine requiring a warning is a visit from your mother."

"Start the sirens," he said. "She'll be here on Monday."

"And how is Enid?" Mary asked, and Ginger could see how hard she was trying not to look pointedly at Ginger.

"She's...on a mission," Sam said, leaning his forearms on the counter. "She intends to get me engaged."

"Oh?" Mary apparently couldn't help herself anymore, and she looked at Ginger, raising her brows. "And is she going to succeed?"

"She'll think she has," Sam assured her. "Mary, this is Ginger Marsh. She'll be playing the part of my fiancée. Ginger, Mary went to school with my mother. She probably knows her better than anyone else."

Ginger gave her a polite smile, coupled with an apologetic shrug of her shoulders. She didn't want this pleasant woman thinking that this bizarre plan was any of her doing.

"Playing the part of your fiancée?" Mary repeated, totally disregarding the rest of his statement. "And what does that mean?"

"It means that Mother wants me to be engaged, so I'll be engaged. Are you going to help us pull this off, or aren't you?"

Mary looked at them both, then looked again. Finally, she began to smile.

"So we're going to put one over on your mother, are we?"

"That's the spirit, Mary," Sam said, grinning. "Now, what have you got in engagement rings that we could rent?"

"Rent?" Mary's brows went up again. "Sweetie, I can do better than that." She held one hand in the air and disappeared into a back room.

"Sam," Ginger said as soon as she was out of earshot, "should we be involving her in this? I mean, she's your mother's friend."

"And she's my godmother," Sam said. "She's

helped me get around my mother's plans more times than I can count. She's never let me down yet.''

"Let me get this straight," she said dryly. "You're not above using your godmother to con your own mother."

"Before you start lecturing me," he said in a low voice, "remember that you're the one accepting the paycheck in this little con game."

Ginger flushed, but before she could retort, Mary returned, beaming.

"Here we go!" she sang out, holding out her palm. Ginger and Sam both leaned forward to see the ring. "It's old," Mary said, "and the setting's loose. I've been meaning to reset the diamond, but I never got around to it. You give me tonight to work on it, and tomorrow you have an engagement ring—on loan."

"It's lovely," Ginger said, admiring the old-fashioned setting. The diamond was small, and it was surrounded by a tiny cluster of even smaller diamonds. "Are you sure we can borrow this?"

"I can't think of a prettier fiancée I'd like to see wearing it," Mary assured her, patting her hand. "It was my mother's, but since I didn't have any children, I had no one to give it to. I'd rather have it be seen on your hand than sit around in a dark desk drawer. Here, let me get your size, honey, and tomorrow you'll have a ring on your finger." She winked at Sam, her eyes sparkling.

Ginger still felt prickly with irritation over Sam's high-handed reminder that she was accepting money to help him fool his mother. She barely spoke to Sam while he taxied her from one errand to another.

From the jewelry store he took her to the grocery

store, where he pushed the cart while she shopped, then paid for the food. From there he took her to her own shop, to pick up a sweeper and other cleaning supplies.

When they were headed back to his ranch, Ginger, who had managed to sit by the passenger window of the truck on the way into town, found herself inexplicably in the middle between Sam and Emily. The supplies and groceries were in the back seat of the extended-cab truck.

The way Sam's shoulder brushed hers was sending shivers down her spine, and when his arm lightly touched hers as he shifted gears, she jerked away as if scorched. Which was how she felt. Equally unsettling were the looks Sam had given her all day, almost as if he were working up the courage to tell her something. But she was so unnerved by his nearness that she couldn't seem to focus on much of anything.

This was *not* supposed to happen, she thought wildly. She had been quite happily married to a gentle, considerate businessman whose closest brush with outdoor activity was watching golf tournaments on TV. There was no way she could be drawn to a muscular, stubborn, arrogant *cowboy* who had practically tried to convince her that she was doing a public service by posing as his fiancée. She was not the kind of woman who was attracted to the Marlboro Man.

And Sam was definitely a cowboy. He might ride a truck instead of a horse, but he was hard-core cowboy down to his bones. He was used to the outdoors and animals and the sheer challenge of making a living from the land. And Ginger knew nothing about any of that.

"You know, I'm still not sure you're the right person to play my fiancée," he said suddenly, as if he were bringing up a problem that had been plaguing him for a while.

"You could send out a casting call," Ginger said dryly. "Although it's a bit late in the game."

"Granted, I'm fighting the time element here," he said. "But I was really hoping for someone more like..." He threw her a frowning glance, unsure how to put this.

"Please go on," she said, in a falsely encouraging voice.

Sam searched his memory for the domestic image he wanted. He'd seen it on a box in his cupboard. It was a brand name. The pancakes.

"Like Betty Crocker," he said, the name suddenly coming to him.

Ginger's brows lifted delicately. "You wanted a cardboard drawing for your fiancée?"

"No, no!" He shook his head in irritation. "What I meant was...someone who looks more at home in the kitchen."

"More at home in the kitchen?" she repeated in exasperation. What was that supposed to mean? "If you recall, I *do* run a catering business."

"I mean, couldn't you at least wear an apron when Mother's here?" he asked. "And maybe a hat or something? You know, to cover your hair."

"An apron and a hat?" she asked, on the verge of being highly insulted. "You want me to wear a waitress's uniform for your mother? Listen, cowboy, you're perilously close to getting your nose punched here."

"Well, I'm not asking you to wear a name tag or anything," he insisted. "Just look a little more... domestic."

Ginger sighed heavily and leaned back against the seat, her eyes closed.

"Why didn't you just hire Julia Child?" she asked in a falsely sweet voice. "I think she meets your qualifications better than I do."

"It's just that you're sort of... Well, you're a little too pretty."

Ginger sat there with her mouth open. Too pretty?

"Well, thank you—I think," she said. "And, believe me, if you want me to run around the house in a tutu and carrying a feather duster, I'll do it. After all, you're the customer."

She slanted a sideways glance at him, pleased to note his apparent discomfort. She was as determined as he was to keep this little production on a business footing. And if he thought he could throw her for a loop with his silly requests, he had another think coming.

She got herself out of the truck as soon as humanly possible once it braked in front of his door. Then she busied herself unloading groceries and supervising Emily.

"We'll make lunch," she told Sam, deliberately not looking at him.

Emily was used to helping her mother, and she started putting the bread and lunch meat and cheese on the table while Ginger eyed the electric can opener on the counter. From the looks of the stains on it, it had opened about a million cans of spaghetti without ever seeing a washrag. Ginger compromised, giving it a quick once-over with some soap and hot water before opening the can of soup. She decided it was enough of a cleaning to stave off any major infections.

Sam hovered at the kitchen door, his hands stuck in his pockets, feeling completely useless. But he did like watching Ginger and her daughter work. She was quick and efficient, and she smiled often at Emily. It struck him that he hadn't seen someone smile in this house for a very long time. He had felt her muscles jerk when he accidentally touched her in the truck, and it had thrown him momentarily off balance. He knew he'd riled her with his request that she look more "domestic," but he didn't want the added distraction of her looks. The sight of her swaying hips and bottom in those jeans was enough to make a man drool.

He forced himself to look away, and for the first time saw the house as Ginger must have seen it on the impromptu tour he gave. There wasn't much here that was appealing. The furniture had never been to his taste. His wife had chosen it, spending a small fortune. Yet she'd left it behind when she was done with the marriage, demanding a cash settlement instead. In her absence, the house had become neglected and shabby.

And so had he, he thought with a flash of regret. He wasn't shabby physically, but inside he felt the way the house looked, unkempt and neglected.

"Did your mother cook when you were growing up?" Ginger asked, gesturing for him to sit down at the table as she got out glasses.

"Not much," he admitted. "She spent most of her evenings with the local amateur theater group. Mother always wanted to be an actress. Although *wanted* is an understatement."

He was waiting at Ginger's chair to hold it for her, and she flushed as she sat down. But he seemed to be thinking about his mother and not concentrating on her. When his hand lightly touched her arm before he moved away, Ginger felt her blood heat.

"Was she on the stage professionally?" Ginger asked, pouring each of them a glass of milk.

Sam shook his head. "To Mother, life is her stage. The more drama she can wring from it, the better."

"She sounds formidable," Ginger said.

"Another understatement," he agreed. "When Mother wants something, she puts all of her considerable will into getting it."

"Like getting you married," Ginger said, smiling in spite of herself. The more she thought about it, the more amused she was by Sam's dilemma, especially after his indignant comments on her appearance. "What do you think your mother will do after she goes home and your engagement doesn't end in a marriage?"

"I'll cross that bridge after I come to it," Sam assured her. "But I have *no* intention of marrying again."

"The strong, silent, solitary type," Ginger offered dryly.

"Who can recognize a city girl a mile away," he countered, regarding her through unreadable eyes. "You're prettier—and flashier—than Denise," he said, "but you're cut from the same cloth. For my sake, I hope you can do a good job of pretending to love the ranch."

"The ranch is no problem," Ginger said flippantly. "The hard part will be making her believe that I love her pigheaded son." She smiled sweetly, and Sam scowled.

"I'd better get busy outside." He picked up his sandwich and headed for the door. He said something under his breath, something that sounded like "Ferrari with an attitude."

She had no idea what that meant.

3

By late afternoon, Ginger had dusted and swept the entire downstairs and most of the upstairs of the house. She had studiously avoided Sam's bedroom, not only because of the skitter of nerves she felt when she passed it, but also because she didn't want to move his belongings. And she would certainly have to clean up that pile of papers, magazines, clothes and odds and ends, if she was to clean the room. Sighing, she put off tackling the room until later.

She sent Emily outside to play, warning her to stay out of Sam's way. Given his jaded view of women, Ginger didn't want Emily to disturb him.

The few curtains in the house were inexpensive and washable, so she took them down and started a load in the washer. Next she tackled the windows, moving systematically from one to the other inside. By the time the curtains went in the dryer, she had almost finished.

The furniture just wasn't right, she thought for the hundredth time as she crossed the living room. Far too sterile and cold. Well, she did have some scrap fabric at the shop. She could whip up a few throw pillows, and she thought she even had enough to do some curtains for the kitchen. That, and a few plants, would cheer up the house immeasurably.

Ginger checked the sink, where she was soaking the stove drip pans. Convinced that it would take another hour—or maybe days—to soak them enough to loosen the burned spillovers, she decided to do the windows from the outside next. It was almost dinnertime now, anyway. She could collect Emily, go eat dinner, and make two or three pillows at home tonight. She had all day tomorrow to finish cleaning and do some extra sprucing-up.

But when she gathered her bucket and spray bottle after finishing the lower level windows on the back of the house, she heard the distinct sound of a softball hitting a glove. She hadn't realized that Emily had brought her ball and glove with them.

"Emily, you'd better be careful," she warned, rounding the corner to the front and pulling up short in surprise.

Emily had just thrown the ball—and Sam, kneeling on the grass, caught it.

It wasn't Emily's softball or her glove, Ginger realized a second later. These had never been used, judging from their new look.

"Where did you get those?" she asked warily.

Emily glanced at Sam before hesitantly saying, "They're Sam's. He said I could try them out."

"They've been gathering dust for a long time," Sam said, but he wouldn't meet Ginger's eyes.

"I'm hungry, Mom," Emily said, "and you promised we could have a picnic today."

"We'll go eat as soon as I'm done with the windows," she said.

"Why don't you eat here?" Sam asked, and Ginger glanced at him again, while trying to come up with some excuse why they couldn't stay. She had thought she had Sam Weller pinned down in her mind and relegated to a place where she could deal with him. But she couldn't keep him pinned down if he kept surprising her like this. She wondered if the ball and glove had been intended for children he'd never had.

"I *did* promise Emily a picnic," Ginger said, by way of explaining why they couldn't stay.

Sam shrugged and pushed his hat back on his head. "So, have the picnic here. I could get out the ladder and finish the upper windows while you get it ready. I have to eat, too, you know," he said. "And you've done enough hard work for today. Let me do the windows." His tone was cool, but Ginger noticed that he wouldn't meet her eyes.

"Well, if you're going to be an ogre about it," she teased him, gratified when he finally gave a half smile. "Come on, Emily. Help me fry some chicken while Sam makes good on his window-washing promise."

"Did you know that Sam has a bicycle in the barn, too?" Emily asked her mother as she leaned her elbows on the counter to watch her cook.

"And what were you doing in Sam's barn?" Ginger asked quickly.

Emily's sneaker toe squeaked on the floor as she swung her leg. She gave her mother a hopeful smile.

"I saw a cat go in there, and I was afraid it might be...stomped by a horse or something. You know how you have to watch out for cats. Did you know that Sam has horses too?"

"More than likely you were watching out for Emily Marsh," Ginger said. "And no, I didn't know that Sam has horses."

Realizing that she wasn't in big trouble for checking out the barn, Emily grinned.

"Sam said I can ride one of the horses sometime. Did you know he never had a bike when he was a kid, so he bought that one?"

"I wonder why he never had a bike...." Ginger mused.

"I asked, and he said his mother didn't buy him one. You know, Mom, I don't think she knew very much about little kids. He said she got him a clarinet when he asked for a bike. Who would buy a clarinet when a kid asked for a bicycle?"

That would be typical of the formidable Enid Weller, Ginger thought. No wonder Sam wasn't about to go find a real wife. He'd probably had enough disappointments from both his mother and his ex-wife to send him running from the female gender.

Well, it wasn't her problem, she told herself. The only thing she had to worry about at the moment was not burning the chicken. Sam had left his hat on the counter while he washed windows, and Ginger pushed it aside to make room. She almost smiled, thinking of him playing catch with Emily. He wasn't as cold as he apparently wanted her to think.

Sam came into the kitchen as Ginger was draining the chicken on paper towels. Ratso was sacked out in the corner, snoring contentedly after Ginger having given him the meat from a fried chicken wing.

"The windows are done," he said. "That smells good."

"We're just about ready," Ginger told him, but Sam noticed that she wasn't looking at him. He wondered if she felt as edgy as he did about this picnic. He was almost sorry he'd told her and Emily to stay. But the disappointment he felt when she said they were leaving had been keener than his discomfort at the prospect of being around her for dinner.

He picked up his hat from the counter and watched her wrap the chicken in foil, then pack it in a large paper grocery bag.

"I think everything's ready," she told him, turning around and busying herself tidying up the counter. She seemed as reluctant to look at him as he was to look at her.

"I'll carry that," he said, stepping forward and reaching for the bag at the same time she did. Their hands touched, their fingers tangled, and Ginger jerked away.

"Be careful," she said, her voice slightly uneven. "Don't burn yourself on the chicken."

And that wasn't the only danger, he decided as he saw the pink flush climb her cheeks. He had a sudden urge to kiss Ginger Marsh, and if Emily hadn't been in the kitchen, he might have done so right then and there, such was the physical effect she had on him. His almost-forty-year-old hormones went into overdrive whenever she was close. And that floored him.

He had felt a physical attraction for a particular woman now and then since his divorce, but mostly he kept his impulses under tight rein. He knew that physical involvement usually led to emotional involvement, and he had no wish to let a woman feel something for him, then tell her that commitment on his part was out of the question.

Swallowing hard, he hefted the bag and silently led the way to the truck. He had to keep his hands off her, he told himself. He would bring both of them nothing but grief if he didn't.

"Where are we going?" Ginger asked as he steered

the truck toward a gate in the pasture behind the house. Ginger had been relieved when Emily climbed into the truck first and claimed the middle seat. She still carried the physical memory of his arm brushing against hers, and just thinking about it sent shivers down her spine again.

"You'll see," Sam said enigmatically, and Ginger sighed. She hoped he wasn't so enamored of his Black Angus cows that they were going to picnic in the middle of the herd, surrounded by manure and flies.

But there were no cattle here, Ginger noticed as the truck bumped along slowly over the grass. What she saw were fruit trees, laden with almost ripe apples— several varieties, from what Ginger could tell.

The truck skirted the grove of trees, coming to rest under the shade of a huge oak tree with a gnarled and thick trunk. Looking past the tree, Ginger could see that the hill where they were stopped sloped down to a good-size lake. It glowed almost lavender in the light of the sun that was slipping below the treeline. The sight nearly took Ginger's breath away. This was what she had dreamed of when she left the city, a peaceful, quiet setting that could soothe the soul.

Although she didn't feel all that soothed with Sam beside her, helping her down from the truck. His hand on her arm started a yearning deep inside her that it would have taken more than a sunset and a lake to alleviate.

And he relinquished her arm quickly, as if touching her weren't something that brought him calm, either.

"Oh, wow, look at that!" Emily cried, pointing toward the lake. "Can I go fishing there, Sam?"

He laughed as he spread the blanket on the ground under the oak tree. "Anytime. There should be some good-size bass in there by now. I stocked it a long time ago.''

Ginger waited for him to elaborate, but he didn't. And he was avoiding looking at her again.

''The apple trees are loaded,'' she commented neutrally.

Sam shrugged. ''I spray them every year, but I don't know why I bother. I never pick the apples.''

But he sprayed the trees. And from the looks of the landscape around her, he kept this piece of land well mowed and cared-for. Maybe he bothered because he still cared, at least a little bit.

''Can we eat now?'' Emily broke in. ''I'm *starved.*''

''All right,'' Ginger said, kneeling on the blanket and unpacking the bag. ''Grab a plate and get started.''

Sam gestured for her to go first, and she did, conscious of his eyes on her as she helped herself to the chicken, baked beans, cheese, fruit and rolls. He was still standing, as if reluctant to actually join her and Emily in this domestic scene.

''Sit down,'' Ginger said to him finally. ''If you eat standing up, you're going to drop baked beans on my head, and then you can't have any dessert.''

''Pretty strict about dessert, aren't you?'' Sam commented, trying to hide his smile.

''Nobody comes between me and my chocolate,'' Ginger assured him.

Emily giggled, and Sam finally sat, arranging himself cross-legged, as Emily and Ginger did. He took off his hat and dropped on the blanket. He still wouldn't look at Ginger as he filled his plate.

They ate in silence, except for the sounds of birds calling from near the lake and an occasional fly buzzing past.

Sam marveled that Ginger had been able to put together this meal so quickly. She had all kinds of talents he hadn't suspected. His mother would approve of her heartily.

Thinking of his mother and her mission only made him morose, but he felt better knowing that the house was almost ready for her. At least he would be spared his mother's not-so-veiled comments about the lack of cleanliness that his bachelorhood existence imposed on the house. And with Ginger cooking, there would be no nightly drives into town to pick up pizza or Chinese or Italian.

Ginger would be there every evening. He realized suddenly that he was looking forward to having her around—but just as a buffer against his mother's meddling.

"Okay if I go skip stones on the lake?" Emily asked around the last bite of the large brownie she was devouring.

Ginger waved her away with a warning to be careful and began closing the plastic containers and returning them to the bag. When she had the last crumb put away in the bag and there was absolutely nothing else for her to do, she folded her hands in her lap and said hesitantly, "It seems a shame to waste the apples. Why don't I get a few to take back?"

She was about to lever herself to her feet when Sam caught her wrist. She looked at him in surprise.

"I just wanted to...thank you for doing this," he said, his own face emotionless.

She was about to tell him that he was more aggravation than he was worth, but she didn't. She gave him a fleeting smile, ready to bolt away from him, because the feel of his fingers at her sensitive pulse point was making the blood pound through her veins. She tilted her head teasingly and asked, ''Did I pass the Betty Crocker cooking test?''

''You may cook like her, but that's as far as the resemblance goes,'' he said firmly.

''Just trying to earn my paycheck, boss,'' she said sassily.

''Ginger...''

He didn't mean to do it, but once he'd touched her soft skin and felt her blood pounding there at her wrist, he couldn't help it. In one swift movement, Sam tugged her sharply toward him, and she landed squarely against his chest, her fingers splayed on his shirt for balance.

She started to protest, but then she was too mesmerized by the sudden change in his face to speak. The harsh lines around his eyes eased, and his expression warmed as he looked down at her. His mouth hovered over hers and, like a moth unable to escape the flame, Ginger strained toward him.

Firm, demanding lips brushed hers, making passion spring to life inside her, coaxing it from her as one would build a fire.

And it was fire that consumed her, licking down her spine and through her limbs, making her lean into the kiss and wind her arms around his neck.

His hand had long ago released her wrist to cradle her head and stroke the side of her throat with a languid thumb. Ginger pressed her breasts against his chest, feeling the responsive shudder that ran through him.

A moment later, his mouth raised, and his hand abruptly left her hair. Ginger could feel the change come over him as surely as she could have felt the wind preceding a rainstorm.

She drew back, staring up at him in confusion. Where there had been warmth a second before, now there was the same guarded expression she'd come to recognize in just a short time. And regret.

He was sorry he had kissed her. That hurt her more than the icy reserve that was back on his face.

"I'm not reading anything into this, if that's what you're thinking," she said quietly, determined not to let him know what the kiss had done to her.

After a long silence, during which conflicting emotions crossed his face, he said, "I was thinking that...my mother will expect us to act like an engaged couple. I wanted to make sure you can handle that."

Ginger sat back on her heels as that sank in. She hadn't given that aspect of their relationship any thought, because she had been so busy thinking about what had to be done to the house. Now, belatedly, she realized that he was right. They would have to make his mother believe that they were in love, and that would of course mean a certain amount of...physical contact. In the next instant, she felt a stab of anger that the kiss had only been an experiment to him.

She cleared her throat uncomfortably.

"If you find it too difficult to pretend to be attracted to me—" he began, but she waved away what he had been about to say. Unfortunately, it was becoming a little too easy to pretend to be attracted to him.

"It's just that... I guess you took me by surprise," she said slowly, trying not to look into his eyes.

"We *will* have to appear to be in love," he reminded her.

"I can manage to act the part," she said sharply, pushing to her feet and brushing imaginary dirt from her jeans.

When he didn't say anything, she turned to look at him, alarmed by the challenging look on his face.

"Are you sure?" he asked in a low voice. "Do you know what you're getting into, Ginger Marsh?"

He was teasing her, but she quickly put some distance between them anyway, moving to pick up the paper bag. She clutched it to her chest as he moved toward her, practically squeezing the life out of the food packed inside. No, she didn't know what she was getting into, and it was beginning to worry her.

"What are you doing?" she demanded when he was a few inches away.

"Just getting those apples you wanted to take back with us," he said with a rumbling laugh. Stepping around her, he bent to scoop up his hat, then headed toward the grove of trees.

Slowly releasing her breath, Ginger lowered her eyes to the bag. She groaned when she saw the leftover rolls, now as flat as pancakes.

Some fiancée she was turning out to be. She had been married for ten years, and here she was, panicking like a skittish cat at the touch of a man.

She had never believed in romance. She had known her husband for years before they married, and theirs had been a quiet love with no raised voices or slammed doors. There had been no earthshaking physical passion either, but Ginger didn't believe that that existed anywhere but in foolish people's imagination.

No, she thought again, she certainly didn't know what she was getting into, but then, maybe he didn't, either.

4

Ginger had just stepped out of the shower and wrapped a towel around her wet hair on Sunday morning when she heard the buzzer ring on the shop door downstairs.

"Drat!" she muttered, pulling on a pair of jeans and a faded sweatshirt she fished out of the dirty clothes hamper.

Most people respected the Closed sign she hung on the door on Sundays, but twice since she opened the shop, someone had come by with a domestic emergency. One middle-aged man had needed a quick gourmet dinner for unexpected company, and a bubbly girl with blond hair had begged for a fast tailoring job on a dress that had fit the month before but mysteriously shrank while hanging in the closet.

Ginger had come to the rescue both times. Not only was it good for business, she was a sucker for a sob story. So whoever was on the other side of her door was likely to get what he or she wanted.

Or maybe not, she thought after looking through the peephole and opening the door.

Sam's blue eyes raked down her front, from the towel about to fall off her head to her wrinkled jeans to her bare feet. Ginger felt her toes curl in embarrassment.

"What are you doing here?" she asked in some annoyance, clutching the towel with her hand.

"Did you forget we're picking up the ring today?" Sam asked, with an equal amount of irritation.

"At...seven-thirty in the morning?" Ginger demanded, having to turn around to consult the clock on the wall over the cash register.

When she turned back, Sam was trying to suppress a smile.

"This is the best time of the day," he assured her. "The air's crisp and clean, and you never know what might happen."

"Right," she said dryly. "Some idiot could knock on your door while you're in the shower."

Sam did smile then, and Ginger was mesmerized by the way it transformed his face. He no longer looked cold or forbidding. No, a smiling Sam Weller was a more youthful and warmer man. And infinitely more dangerous to her libido. She could still feel the kiss he had given her the day before, as if it had left an indelible imprint.

"Do you have to wear such sexy jeans?" he demanded, the smile gone as quickly as it had appeared.

There was that irrational complaint again about her lack of plainness. She would have hit him, if both her hands weren't occupied preventing the towel falling off her head.

"You forget," she said dryly, "that I'm the anti–Betty Crocker. It'll save me having to answer a lot of your aggravating questions if you'd keep that in mind."

"I will," he assured her, and it looked as if he were almost smiling again.

"Well," she said briskly, "come on upstairs, and I'll get ready. There's coffee on."

Sam followed her, trying not to stare at her curvaceous hips and the trim bottom that wiggled ever so slightly as she climbed the stairs in front of him.

"Is it hot?" he asked suddenly. "The coffee, I mean," he said, clearing his throat and looking at everything in the small apartment except Ginger.

"I think I can guarantee that," Ginger said, amused by his obvious discomfort. "The cups are in the cupboard over the stove, and there are some doughnuts on the counter."

When Ginger got back to the kitchen, having awakened Emily, dressed, and towel-dried her hair, she heard Emily inform Sam, "Now, if you put the fork in here and then just lift up a little, you can tell what kind it is."

They both looked up guiltily as Ginger came into the kitchen, Emily hastily dropping the fork onto her napkin.

"Sam doesn't like boysenberry jelly," Emily announced.

"So you decided to inspect each and every doughnut on his behalf?" Ginger asked, sighing as she held up a sugared doughnut that bore numerous fork-induced punctures. "My daughter, the doughnut poker."

Emily giggled. For his part, Sam could barely take his eyes off Ginger. Her hair hung in lush, damp waves of honeyed gold and copper around her face. A green T-shirt was tucked into neatly tapered blue jeans that hugged her hips where a man's hand would naturally come to rest if he was holding her against him.

Sam abruptly broke off that unproductive chain of thought and swallowed the last of his coffee.

Catching him eyeing her outfit, Ginger suppressed a smile.

"I almost forgot," she said, reaching into her purse, which sat on the floor. When she straightened, Sam saw that she had fastened her hair back into a ponytail. "Does this look more domestic?" she asked innocently.

"We'd better go before Mary leaves for her Sunday-morning coffee klatch," Sam said gruffly, noting that the ponytail did nothing to tone down her appearance.

Ginger hid her smile and took a long swallow of coffee before turning off the automatic coffeemaker. She grabbed one last doughnut and hurried after Sam and her daughter. It seemed that everyone in this town sprang into action at the crack of dawn on the weekends.

Mary Stafford was waiting for them, unlocking the door as soon as the truck stopped in front of the store.

She ushered them inside and immediately took the ring from the back office. Ginger started to reach for it, but Mary had already handed it to Sam.

He looked at it a moment, his face unreadable, then held out his hand for Ginger's. She gave him her left hand, swallowing around the lump in her throat as he slipped the ring onto her finger. He held her hand for a long moment, then looked up at Mary and smiled.

"It's perfect," he said, the warmth in his eyes belying the roughness of his voice.

"Let me see!" Emily pleaded, and Ginger took the opportunity to quickly extricate her hand from Sam's and hold it out for her daughter to admire.

Emily gave a low whistle. "It sparkles," she said.

"Just like your eyes. Right, Sam? Isn't that what you told me?"

Ginger could have sworn that Sam was blushing as he jammed his cowboy hat lower on his face and mumbled something in reply.

"Anybody want an ice cream cone?" he asked gruffly.

"Me! Me!" Emily cried.

"Sam, it's eight-thirty in the morning," Ginger protested. "Nobody eats ice cream that early."

"Emily and I do," he told her, still not meeting her eyes.

Mary Stafford was watching the whole transaction with amusement.

"Honey," she told Ginger, "if you're going to be engaged to Sam Weller, even if it's a temporary engagement, you've got to be prepared for the unusual." She winked at Emily.

"Well, I guess it's time for ice cream, then," Ginger said, giving in, even though she knew that it was a ploy of Sam's to get Emily off the subject of Ginger's supposedly *sparkling* eyes.

To Ginger's amazement, the ice cream shop two stores up the street from the jeweler's was actually open. Once inside, Ginger saw that the place served doughnuts, sweet rolls and juice, as well as ice cream—reason enough to be open during breakfast hours.

The bridal store next to the ice cream shop was still closed, and Ginger felt grateful for that. Otherwise, he would probably have her in there picking out a dress to further convince his mother of the engagement.

Emily wanted a strawberry cone and immediately retreated to a nearby chair to savor it. Ginger tried to demur when Sam asked what she wanted, but he insisted.

"Mrs. Marsh," he said, leaning close and thumbing the cowboy hat back on his head, "a woman who won't eat ice cream when it's offered is suspect in this part of the country."

Ginger tried not to smile. "Suspect of what?" she demanded.

"Of not having any fun," Sam assured her. "She might even be the type who won't dance or play cards."

"Heaven forbid I be suspected of that kind of behavior," Ginger said with feigned horror. "All right, I'll have a double fudge ripple."

"There you go," Sam told her, a smile hovering around his mouth. "A double. I like a woman who can hold her ice cream."

"You think I'm good with ice cream?" she said confidentially. "You should see me with fudge."

Sam laughed then, and Ginger found herself mesmerized again. He had a rich, deep laugh that started as a chuckle in his throat and expanded into a rumble from his chest that lit up his blue eyes.

He truly was a good-looking man, Ginger thought appreciatively. And sexy as hell.

The girl behind the counter handed Sam his own ice cream, a double dip of rocky road, then smiled at Ginger.

"Congratulations," she said, nodding toward the ring on Ginger's finger.

"Oh, we're not—" Ginger began, but Sam smoothly cut her off.

"Setting the date for a couple of months yet," he said. "Come on, honey. We'd better get back to the house." He put his hand on Ginger's waist and guided her to the door.

"I'm sorry," she said in consternation as soon as they were outside and Emily had run ahead of them to the truck. "I wasn't thinking."

"No harm done," Sam said, his hand leaving her waist as he searched his pocket for his keys. But his voice was noticeably cooler, and Ginger wondered how he could return so quickly to his usual brusque demeanor. He helped her into the truck, and she sighed as he went around to the other side. After he slid into the seat beside her, he barely glanced at her before he scowled at the road. Ginger stifled another sigh and bit into her ice cream cone.

She spent the morning sewing some simple throw pillows, using the scrap fabric and her portable sewing machine she had asked Sam to load in the truck when they left her shop. Emily sat on the porch, reading the book she had brought along.

Sam had disappeared as soon as they got to the house, and Ginger heard the faint sounds of a tractor engine from somewhere in the distance. He had appeared briefly at lunchtime, grabbing a sandwich but turning down the soup she'd heated to go with it. He'd taken two bites and headed back out the door, eating as he went.

"No need to panic, cowboy," Ginger had muttered to no one in particular. "I have no intention of putting my brand on you anyway."

Ginger clipped the last thread from the red-and-white checkered curtains she'd sewn and carried them to the kitchen. They were of a simple design, not much more than hemming two square pieces of fabric, but when she slipped them over the curtain rod, they cheered the kitchen immediately. Using her small battery-operated hand drill, she installed a hook on each side of the window, then tied the curtains back with matching fabric trimmed in red rickrack.

Satisfied with the results, she headed upstairs to work on Sam's bedroom. She'd been putting that off all morning, but it was time to enter the lion's den.

There was a radio on the night table beside the bed, and she turned it on, finding a station with old rock music. The upbeat tempo and driving beat helped her work faster.

She scooped up every paper, magazine—most of them were agricultural publications on cattle ranching, she noticed—and receipt, straightening the pile as best she could, then tucking it away in a corner of his closet. The closet itself was relatively bare, and that gave her enough room to hang each piece of clothing she found strewn on the bed or floor.

Much better, she thought as she stood back and dusted her hands. She tackled the dresser next, dusting and straightening. She found a small white pitcher hidden behind some framed family photos, and she filled it with water, then went outside to cut some of the wild blue asters and white yarrow that grew beside Sam's pasture fence.

That done, Ginger went back to dusting the photos, unable to help noticing one nearly hidden in the back—a smiling Sam with a woman in a broad-brimmed hat and a sundress. Her hand was on the hat to hold it on, and they were standing by a lake, possibly the lake on Sam's property. The woman was staring straight into the camera, her face purposeful and a little flirtatious. His ex-wife, she imagined.

Ginger put the picture down, then picked it up again when she saw a piece of fabric hanging from the back of the dresser. She pulled it up, frowning when she saw that it was a woman's slip, white and lacy.

With the radio on, she didn't hear Sam come up the stairs, and she jumped when he said, "Throw it out."

"What?" she said as she turned around, pressing the hand holding the slip to her chest.

"Throw that thing out," he said. "Denise took everything she valued when she left."

His eyes fell to the photo Ginger still clutched in her other hand, along with the dustcloth and polish, and his jaw tightened.

"What are you doing with that?" he demanded.

"I was just cleaning," Ginger began, afraid he thought she had been snooping in his bedroom. She didn't know what to put down first, and in her agitation, the bottle of polish began to slip from her hand. Ginger clutched at it, but then she lost her grip on the picture, and it fell to the carpet with a soft thud, the bottle of polish landing on top.

"Oh, Sam, I'm sorry," she murmured as she knelt and saw the crack in the glass. She touched the glass, then pressed her fingers to her lips in consternation.

He was kneeling beside her in the next instant, pulling her hand from her face.

"Did you cut yourself?" he asked, in obvious concern. "I'm sorry, Ginger. I didn't mean to yell at you."

"It's all right," she said, her hand trembling slightly as he inspected her fingers. "You just startled me."

"Are you sure you're all right?" he asked, his brow furrowed, his thumb absently stroking her palm.

Ginger nodded, her blood pounding in her throat.

"I'll replace the glass," she told him. "The picture is still intact."

"Damn the picture!" he said vehemently. "Throw it out. I'm tired of seeing it."

Ginger stared at him in surprise. "But I thought... You seemed angry that I was holding it."

Sam dropped her hand finally, leaving her skin feeling parched for his touch. He raked a hand through his hair. For once, the cowboy hat was missing.

"I get mad at myself every time I see that picture. I was thirty-two when I got married, not some dumb kid. I should have known better. I should have seen what I was getting into. That I was messing with a woman who didn't want me, or this place."

"Why did she marry you, then?" Ginger asked boldly.

"Because she thought I was a way of getting the things she wanted. Because she probably watched too much TV and thought 'Dallas' showed the reality of cattle ranching. Swimming pools and fancy clothes and big cars, that was what Denise wanted."

Ginger shook her head. "If you had guessed all that beforehand," she told him, "you could open your own psychic hot line. Believe me, marriage is always full of surprises."

Sam studied her for a moment. "Is that how yours was?" he asked. "Full of surprises?"

Ginger started to give him an easy answer, to say yes, and most of the surprises were good. But she made herself stop and consider. He had been honest with her, and she owed him the truth.

"That's the hard part of marriage," she said carefully. "Learning to accept the things you might like to change about someone else. I guess that was the biggest surprise for me. Realizing that I loved someone enough to let him be himself.''

Sam continued to study her, and she felt herself begin to flush under his scrutiny. She realized that they were still kneeling on the floor, with the radio playing loudly behind them. It was totally incongruous with the conversation they were having.

"You knew your husband well before you were married?'' Sam asked.

Ginger nodded. ''We went to the same school in St. Louis. We'd probably seen each other's best and worst.''

"And what was his worst, Ginger?'' he asked, his eyes holding hers.

Ginger lifted her shoulders in a soft sigh. ''I don't know. He left his clothes on the floor. And he always forgot what I'd asked him to pick up at the store.''

Sam gave a derisive snort. ''Is that all? I think his death has clouded your memory. There are a thousand little things about a man that make up his worst. And a woman, too. That doesn't even count the more important things. You have a convenient memory. But, unlike you, I can remember every angry word Denise ever exchanged with me, every fight, every slammed door. I make myself remember them, Ginger. Because I don't ever want to make that kind of mistake again. My marriage was hell, and I won't let myself forget it.''

Ginger stared at him, wide-eyed, as he levered himself to his feet and stood looking down at her. ''On second thought, don't throw out that picture. It will help me remember why I won't get involved with anyone again.''

Ginger sat on the floor and sighed as his steps echoed down the stairs. She looked down at the picture, at the smiling man Sam had once been, when he was in love. Before the "hell" that his marriage had become.

5

*T*he man was a nutcase, Ginger told herself brusquely
as she finished cleaning Sam's bedroom. He played
good-cop-bad-cop all by himself. First he was tender
and considerate, worrying that she might have cut her
hand, and the next instant he was berating her for a
supposedly faulty memory where her own marriage
was concerned.

He truly was the Marlboro Man—on too much caf-
feine. She couldn't stop thinking of him as a modern-
day cowboy. And if he kept provoking her, she was
liable to turn his hat inside out—while he was wearing
it.

Well, the bedroom looked pretty presentable now,
she decided, stepping back to admire her work. She
had hidden away all of Sam's papers and magazines,
and the furniture and mirror gleamed. But that dingy
blanket on the bed had to go. The bed needed a new
spread, as did the bed in the guest room.

Ginger took a deep breath and frowned. That meant
a trip to the store, and her car was still at home.

She found Emily dusting the banisters and told her
to go wash her hands, then meet her outside to run an
errand.

Well, she thought philosophically, she couldn't irritate Sam much more than she had already.

Then again, maybe she could.

He was scowling when she found him carrying some barbed wire and cutters from the barn. Ginger quickly stepped out of his path and cleared her throat.

"What?" he demanded, halting in his tracks.

"If this is a bad time..." she said, glancing pointedly at his armload.

"It's always a bad time where that bull of mine is concerned," he muttered. "Second time this month he's managed to break through the fence."

"Well, you know what they say," she offered dryly. "The grass is always greener on the other side of the fence."

He didn't seem the least bit amused by that, and Ginger sighed.

"Actually, I was wondering if you could drive me home to pick up my car," she said.

"Why?"

That took her aback.

"Because I need it," she snapped, deciding she could be as ornery as he could.

"Use my truck," he told her, setting down the wire and fishing in his pocket for keys.

"Your truck?" She cast a nervous, sidelong glance at it. "It's stick-shift, isn't it?"

"So?" he returned, with a raise of his brows.

"I haven't driven a stick shift since high school," she said impatiently. "I might break its little gears or something."

"I'll worry about its *little gears*," he said. "Come on."

It was either follow him or stand there and stare

down at the barbed wire he'd abandoned. Sighing, Ginger decided to follow. When he stopped at the truck and opened the driver's-side door, Ginger brightened.

"This won't take long," she assured him, starting to walk to the other side. "You can drop me off at my place and come right home. Emily will be out in a minute."

She stopped walking when she glanced over her shoulder and noticed that he was still standing where she had left him, his hands on his hips. Sam shook his head.

"You're driving," he told her.

His insistence on her driving the truck was beginning to grate on her nerves, but, instead of repeating that she wasn't that accomplished with a stick shift, she gave a weary sigh and climbed into the truck behind the wheel. She faced forward stonily.

She turned her head when she heard him jangling the keys. He held them out with a raised brow, then dropped them into her palm when she offered it.

Ginger stuck the keys into the ignition and turned them. There was a rumble as the engine started, but then the truck bucked, and the engine immediately died. She heard Sam give a painful sigh.

"How many pedals are there on the floor?" he demanded.

"What?"

"Just answer."

Ginger looked down and said, "Three," in a voice that clearly intimated that it was a stupid question.

"And what is the one on the far left?"

Ginger was about to tell him what he could do with those pedals when she realized the point he was making. "Oh!" she said suddenly. "The clutch!" She turned to shoot him an accusing look. "I told you it was a long time."

"Obviously," he said dryly. "Try again." He nodded toward the ignition.

Ginger stretched her leg out to depress the clutch. This time, the truck started and remained in place.

Emily came running from the house, calling, "Wait for me!"

Ginger leaned out the window. "Just wait there a minute, honey, until I get the hang of this."

She pushed a stray lock of hair out of her eyes to scrutinize the gearshift knob. Reverse was all the way to the right and down. Ginger grasped the knob and slid it to the right, then down. Concentrating, she eased her foot from the clutch as she fed the truck gas. It lurched once, but she pressed the clutch back in a bit and tried again. Again the truck bucked, and Ginger gritted her teeth.

"This truck is a lot like you," she muttered to Sam. "Difficult."

"You aren't going to swear, are you?" he asked, with obvious interest.

"No, I'm not going to swear. What gave you that idea?"

She glanced at him and then looked again. She thought he was about to smile.

"It's just that I haven't heard you swear yet." There was the beginning of a smile again. "I just wondered what it would take to make you do that. You seem so...innocent."

"Innocent?" She was so surprised that she let the clutch out too fast and killed the engine again. She closed her eyes and took a deep breath. "I am *not* going to swear," she told him.

"Good for you," he said, with a cheerfulness that made her think he might be close to smiling again.

"All right," she said, opening her eyes and carefully maneuvering the truck in first gear. She came to a stop and looked at him pointedly. "I'm leaving now."

"Can you work the lights?" he asked.

"What for? It's still daylight."

"And it might rain." He nodded toward the west. "You never know. You might need them."

Ginger gripped the wheel and shot him a sidelong glance. "Okay," she said. She began a covert search for the windshield wipers and lights. Sam watched her a moment as she fiddled with the controls on either side of the steering wheel before he reached across the wheel to flip the control.

As the lights came on, Sam withdrew his hand, and his arm brushed Ginger's breasts. Ginger jerked backward as Sam froze. She could feel her heart thudding in her chest like a jackhammer in an earthquake. Heat spread over her skin, climbing to her face. She felt like a silly teenager, her breath shaky, her insides trembling. She'd been married, for heaven's sake. She was no stranger to a man's touch.

But somehow this was different.

Sam removed his arm and cleared his throat gruffly. "Think you can handle it now?" he asked, then cleared his throat again. "The truck?"

"The truck. Right." She swallowed. "I can handle it. The truck, I mean."

Sam opened the door and got out without another word. Ginger stared straight ahead as he called to Emily that her mother was ready, then helped her up into the seat.

"Oh, one other thing," Ginger said, leaning out the

window and deliberately not meeting his eyes. "Could you dig me a little flower bed there to the side of the steps? I want to put in some herbs."

"Yeah," he said, in almost a grunt, and Ginger withdrew her head.

Sam stood in the drive, watching them leave, his hat pulled low over his eyes, his arms folded over his chest. He could still feel the prickles of heat along his arm. He was surprised by his reaction to the accidental touch. All rational thought had fled. He had had another of those tormenting images of how sweet Ginger Marsh would look in his bed.

"Do you think Sam will like this one?" Emily asked anxiously as Ginger put the bedspread on the counter. It was actually a quilt, a blue-and-white log-cabin pattern with matching pillow shams. Ginger looked down at Emily, who was holding the spread they had bought for the other bed, a soft yellow chenille.

"What do you think?" Ginger asked, seeing the earnest concentration in her daughter's face.

"Well, I don't know," Emily said. "It's pretty, but he's so..."

"So what, honey?" Ginger asked.

"He's such a *boy*," Emily concluded, shrugging her shoulders.

Ginger held back her grin. Sam was all male, all right.

"I just thought maybe he wants something with horses or cars or junk like that," Emily said.

Ginger nodded. "I see. Tell you what. Why don't you go get that horse picture you were eyeing over there by the lamps? We'll put that above Sam's bed."

"Neat!" Emily cried, rushing off to get the picture.

And while Emily was retrieving the picture, Ginger idly looked at the party supplies next to the greeting cards. One of the caps caught her eye, and she mischievously put it on the counter next to the bedspread.

"Someone hitting a big one?" the middle-aged female clerk asked conversationally as she turned away from the quilt and rang up the black cap with Older than Dirt emblazoned on it.

"Yes," Ginger said. "Though I think his head turned forty several years before his body."

The clerk glanced at her over her glasses, but said nothing more, as Emily returned with the picture. Ginger paid for the things herself, figuring she could bill Sam for them later.

She and Emily were on their way out of the domestics department when one last thing caught her eye. Laughing, she picked up the frilly apron and headed for the counter again.

"What's that for, Mom?" Emily asked, puzzled.

"It's for Betty Crocker," Ginger said, her eyes alight.

The flower bed was dug, Ginger noticed when she pulled the truck into the driveway. But she didn't see Sam around anywhere, which was just as well. She didn't need another reminder of how addled his touch made her.

Shopping for the bedspreads had lightened Ginger's mood considerably. Humming to herself, she left Emily downstairs to set the table for dinner while she carried the packages upstairs.

She deposited the chenille spread in the guest bedroom, then carried everything else to Sam's room. The picture would look nice over the bed, she thought again as she pulled it out. There were a couple of things she'd picked up for the bathroom, and she fished them from the bag.

Ginger peeled the prices off the soap dish and the toothbrush holder. Carrying the two items in one hand, she opened the bathroom door and started to step inside.

She stepped back quickly, heat climbing to her face. Sam stood poised just beside the shower, a thick white towel wrapped around his slim hips, in the act of drying his hair with another towel. He stared back at her.

For a moment, she couldn't breathe. He was magnificent in his jeans and shirt, but without them...

His chest was hard and covered with dark hair that feathered down his flat stomach to the top of the towel and lower. His muscular arms and shoulders were frozen in the air, the towel in the grip of his long, lean fingers.

''I...'' she began haltingly. Realizing that her eyes had lingered a tad too long on that lower towel, she quickly backed up and closed the door.

What had she been about to say? she berated herself in the bedroom. *I'd like to see what you look like without that towel.* That would have been honest, if not wise.

She hurried to gather up her purse and head back downstairs before he came out of the bathroom.

Too late, she realized with a sinking heart as the bathroom door opened. Ginger turned her back and pretended to study the horse print she'd leaned against the opposite wall.

''Does that go in here?'' Sam asked, and Ginger nodded.

"Emily picked it out for you."

"It's nice."

"She'll be happy to hear that." *Could she have said anything more mundane?* She was too embarrassed to collect her thoughts.

"Ginger? You can turn around now. I'm wearing clothes."

She wondered whether she was imagining the note of amusement in his voice. "That's okay," she assured him. "I don't need to look." That hadn't come out right, either.

His throaty chuckle made her mad. He had no right to make fun of her!

"Don't you dare laugh at me!" She spun toward him, her eyes shooting sparks.

"I'm not laughing at you," he assured her, but his mouth was still quirked up in a smile.

She tried not to notice the way his clean denim shirt clung to his still-damp skin, and the fact that he hadn't closed the top button on his jeans. His feet were bare.

"Then what's so funny?" she demanded, her arms folded across her chest.

"I can't believe that at the ripe old age of forty, I can make a woman run screaming from the sight of me half-dressed." He stepped to the dresser and ran a brush through his hair.

"I did not scream," she protested. "And you're not forty yet."

"Ah, well, then I suppose I can look forward to things going downhill even faster after my next birthday."

"I'm sure there will be a lot more screaming," she assured him. "On your part, if no one else's."

"You think so?" he asked, the amusement still in his voice.

"I think you're the only person who thinks you're old."

"Wait until you hear my mother on that subject," he warned her. Impatiently he ran his hand through his wet hair, ruining whatever order the brush had imposed. "She says age is an attitude, not a number. And she thinks my attitude makes me about seventy-five."

"More like eighty," Ginger said tartly. She almost smiled, thinking of the cap she'd bought for him. "You sure are a cranky old guy, Weller," she told him. Although she couldn't quite think of him as anywhere near old while he was standing there in those jeans. He looked like he'd just stepped off the pages of a men's cologne ad, with his tousled dark hair and hard-muscled torso.

"I'd like to have known you when you were in your twenties," she said suddenly. "I bet you were a real hell-raiser. Fast cars, fast women?" she guessed wryly. She leaned against the end of the bed, interested in what he would say.

"A little of both," he admitted. "I used to tune up my car in the driveway—at odd hours of the night. My father was a rancher, and he claimed that the cattle weren't getting any sleep for all my hot-rodding."

"And the girls?" Ginger prompted him. She hid a smile when she saw that he was starting to blush. She couldn't believe it—the Marlboro Man was sensitive on the subject of women, especially women from his past.

Sam cleared his throat uncomfortably and shifted his position until he was leaning forward with his hands braced on the dresser, his eyes on the wood instead of Ginger.

"I had my share of girlfriends," he said.

"And?" she said. "Don't leave me dangling here, Sam."

He spared her a dry glance, but continued. "They were girlfriends, that's all. At least until Denise."

Ginger frowned. "And she didn't want to live on a ranch once she found out what it was like."

"Right." Sam straightened and turned to look at Ginger. "No woman does."

"Well, your mother was different, wasn't she?" Ginger pointed out.

"Hell, that's an understatement," Sam snorted. Then his mouth tightened. "But if you mean about the ranch, you're wrong. Mother never stayed here more than five days at a time. She said she couldn't think straight, with all the strange noises. Birds, cows, crickets, they all annoyed her. She kept an apartment in town and spent the rest of her time visiting friends in Chicago. Until Dad died. Then she moved to Hawaii."

No wonder Sam believed no woman would live voluntarily on the ranch, Ginger realized. From his mother to his wife, none had been willing to do it so far.

"Did your dad own the ranch when he met your mother?" she asked, unable to contain her curiosity.

Sam nodded, folding his arms and leaning back against the dresser. "Mom was waitressing in a little place outside of Chicago when Dad stopped in for coffee after a cattle-buying trip to Indiana. He said he had his eye on her from the start, and every time he came through after that, he made a point to stop in. He claimed she was impressed with him from the first. She always said he was big and handsome, but too much of a cowboy for her.'' Sam smiled ruefully. "They were opposites in every way, but they got married despite it all."

"But they were happy, weren't they?" Ginger persisted, unwilling to believe that the waitress and the cowboy hadn't been able to make a go of it. They had produced Sam and Jeannie, after all.

"I didn't see many happy times between them when I was a kid," Sam said. "There was at least one fight a day when Mother was staying here."

Ginger sighed. She was becoming increasingly worried about meeting the formidable Enid Weller. Trying to sneak a phony engagement past Sam's mother was beginning to look like a job for Mata Hari, not Ginger Marsh.

"You know," Sam said, "that reminds me of something we'd better settle now."

"What's that?" Ginger watched him warily.

"Don't look so suspicious," he told her. "I'm only thinking that we need to come up with a plausible explanation for how we met. Mother will ask, and we'd better have our story straight."

Ginger's shoulders sagged. She hadn't thought of that.

"Couldn't we just say we ran into each other in the store?" she suggested.

"Mother will want details," he assured her.

"All right," she said blithely. "It was between the oranges and the bananas."

Sam raised a skeptical brow, and Ginger sighed. "Okay, what do you have in mind?"

"My sister Jeannie was trying to get us together on a blind date a month ago. I thought we could just change the time line and tell Mother that Jeannie got us together three months ago, and we took it from there.'' He smiled. ''I can guarantee that Jeannie will confirm our story.''

''You didn't want to go out with me?'' Ginger asked, sounding affronted.

''I didn't know what a great truck driver you were,'' he said, teasing her.

''That's hardly reassuring.'' She crossed her arms and tapped her foot. ''You're the man who wanted to marry Betty Crocker.''

''I just wanted to be engaged to her,'' he corrected her, hiding his smile. ''Marriage was never part of it.''

''So we had a blind date, then?'' she asked, deciding not to get into the murky area of his marriage phobia.

''Back in June,'' he said. ''And it was a roaring success.''

''Where did we go?'' she asked, wondering what he would actually do on a real date.

Sam considered a moment. ''We went out to eat. At the Barge.''

Ginger shook her head. ''Won't work. We've never been there together. And if your mother wants to eat there, it might make her suspicious that no one knows us as a couple.''

Sam frowned. ''Okay, okay. We didn't go there.'' He sank into thought, his brow furrowed, his hand absently rubbing his chin. ''We went...fishing!'' he said suddenly, grinning. ''My lake. I invited you out here, and we went fishing.''

''What did we catch?'' she asked.

Sam frowned at her. ''Mother won't be interested in how many fish we caught.''

''Maybe not, but I am. Now, come on here. What did we catch?''

Sam sighed. "All right. You caught a sunfish, and I got a largemouth bass."

"How come you get to catch the bigger fish?" she demanded.

"Because you looked so cute reeling in that little sunfish," he told her, a sly smile playing around his mouth. "Come on. Let's get some dinner started. All this talk about fishing makes me hungry."

"So what did I use for bait?" she asked, following him out of the room.

"Worms," he called over his shoulder.

"Worms?! Oh, come on. You can do better than that."

"All right. Grasshoppers." He was already down the stairs and headed into the kitchen, but Ginger could have sworn she heard laughter in his voice.

"I want exotic bait," she said, hurrying after him. "Some old cheese, or anchovies."

"All right, here's the deal," he told her when she caught up to him. He was leaning back against the sink, and the sun glinted off his dark hair, giving him a glowing aura. Over his shoulder, Ginger could see Emily playing catch with herself in the yard. "You caught a giant tuna right there in my lake, and you were using chocolate truffles on a hook with a rod and reel," Sam said. "The tuna fought like hell, but you subdued him by questioning him to death."

She could see that he was just barely holding in a grin.

"Did we have the tuna stuffed?" she teased him.

He dived for her, and Ginger squealed as he caught her around the waist and hauled her against him. There was definite laughter in his eyes now, and Ginger went still in his arms, losing herself in those blue depths.

"You drive me crazy," he whispered, and before she could ask another question, he dipped his head and brushed her mouth with his lips. She responded immediately, her hands going to his chest to clutch his shirt. He raised his head to look at her and seemed on the verge of kissing her again, but then a change came over his face. His eyes darkened, and the laughter was gone as quickly as it had appeared.

"Let's get dinner going," he said in a neutral voice.

As he turned away, Ginger felt an aching twinge of disappointment.

6

Ginger loaded her car in front of her shop early on
Monday morning, ready to put the finishing touches on
things at Sam's ranch before his mother's arrival. She
packed the small decorative pillows she'd stitched the
night before, as well as the perennial plants and herbs
she'd gotten from Mrs. Turner. She sniffed appreciatively at the small white box of fudge she'd also bought
from Mrs. Turner.

Because of a conference that had preempted school
that day, Emily was going with her. Ginger did a mental inventory as Emily climbed into the front seat. She
had already delivered the frothy triple-layer cake and
bottle of champagne another client had ordered to celebrate his wife's birthday today. Ginger smiled as she
remembered how their kitchen had looked. The husband had taken his wife to a local motel the night before, and they would be returning in an hour or so,
before they had to go to work. He had left the key
under the mat for Ginger. Inside, Ginger had seen a
single rose in a bud vase with a card propped beside
it. She had smiled wistfully as she put the cake on the
table and the champagne in the refrigerator.

It would be nice to have a husband who made a

grand gesture, and not just for her birthday. Just once, she would like to be swept off her feet.

She shouldn't complain, she told herself. She'd had good years with Clay.

"Do you think Sam's mother will wear one of those hula skirts?" Emily asked suddenly.

"I don't think so, honey," Ginger said, trying not to smile. That would certainly make this whole charade even more ludicrous.

"Sam said she's coming from Hawaii, and I saw a picture of people wearing those skirts there. And Sam said she likes to dance."

"I think she must like to dance all those regular dances that other people do," Ginger assured her.

"I don't think Sam likes to dance," Emily said. She sighed. "I asked him about it last night while he and I were doing the dishes."

Ginger had gone upstairs to vacuum the carpets in the bedroom when Sam assured her that he and Emily could clean up after supper.

"What did he say?" Ginger asked, hoping the question sounded casual.

"Well, you know how the radio was playing? I asked him if he was going to dance with you sometime. And he said no. He said that..." Emily scrunched up her mouth, trying to remember the words exactly. "He said that a woman who couldn't work a clutch probably couldn't dance. What's a clutch, Mom?"

A clutch was what Ginger wanted to do with her hands and Sam's neck at that moment.

"It's something on a truck," Ginger said with deadly calm. *That conceited cowboy!* She drew in a deep breath, realizing that she had been insulted not once, but twice, the first time on her driving skills and the second on her dancing. Come to think of it, about the only compliment he'd given her since they met was when he said she was too pretty to pass for his domestic-minded fiancée.

He should have hired Betty Crocker for the job, after all, Ginger thought with a mental groan. Should have cut her right off the pancake box and mailed her to his mother.

Ginger's mood didn't improve when she pulled into the ranch. Sam was standing on the porch drinking a cup of coffee, Ratso lying stretched out at his feet. Just seeing him irritated her all over again.

"Hi, Sam!" Emily called cheerfully as she bounded up the steps with the pillows. "Hey, Ratso, want to chase rabbits today?" Ratso opened one eye and sighed, and Emily raced on into the house.

Ginger got the box of plants from the car and carried it to the flower bed Sam had dug for her.

"Want some coffee?" he asked from the porch.

"No, thank you," she said, pulling on her gardening gloves without looking at him. She made another trip to the car, retrieving her trowel. She knelt in front of the bed and began diligently spacing the plants.

Sam came down the steps and stood next to where she knelt.

"Are you sure you don't want any coffee?"

Ginger shook her head. "Had some."

Sam's frown deepened. "Fine." He stalked back up the steps and disappeared inside the house.

Ginger felt a momentary surge of guilt. He was a proud man, and she'd instinctively known that he wouldn't come right out and ask her what was wrong. The offer of coffee was the closest he would come to an overture.

The sun was still slanted low, and it heated her face as she dug in the flower bed. Ginger wiped her forehead with the back of her hand, then went to her car. She had intended to tease Sam with the cap, but the way things were going, she wasn't inclined to present him with it at this point. She plopped it on her own head and went back to work. It was too big, but she was too busy to bother adjusting it at the moment.

An hour later, she had the plants in the bed and was watering them with a hose she had found in the barn. She had sent Emily to the backyard with a book to read. Ginger didn't want to have to do major cleanup on both herself and her daughter before Enid's arrival.

Sam came walking toward her from the field, but Ginger kept her eyes on the plants. She could feel her heartbeat speeding up as he got closer. The cowboy hat was pushed low over his face.

He stopped beside her and stared down at the plants.

"I have to warn you, I don't fuss over plants," he said. "And if these are delicate, they're not going to last long."

"They're not delicate," she said testily. "They're like you. They thrive on neglect. Believe me, they'll grow to gargantuan proportions around here."

Sam's frown deepened. Apparently, a change in subject was in order. "I've been thinking," he said. "We need to come up with a story about how I proposed."

Ginger shrugged. "You asked, and, like a fool, I said yes."

He ignored her sarcasm. "We need a time and place."

"The bowling alley at noon. I don't care."

Sam felt his temper rising, but he bit it back down.

"How about over a picnic lunch by the lake?"

Ginger shrugged again. ''Fine.''

There was a long, uncomfortable silence, during which Sam tried to decide what to say next. Something was obviously irritating her, but despite an hour's thought on the matter, he couldn't come up with a likely cause.

''You know,'' he said finally, ''if you keep giving me the cold shoulder like this, I might get my feelings hurt.''

Ginger tossed down the hose, making him jump back to avoid getting sprayed, and went to the side of the house to turn off the water. When she returned, he was still standing there, his face impassive.

''You should have thought of that when you were busy hurting *my* feelings,'' she said stiffly.

''How did I do that?'' He sounded genuinely surprised.

''You want the complete list, or just the most recent example?'' she retorted.

''It's not that Betty Crocker thing again, is it?'' he asked.

Ginger gave an exasperated sigh. ''This has nothing to do with Betty Crocker. This has to do with dancing.''

He still didn't get it. ''And?'' he prompted her.

''You told Emily that a woman who couldn't remember to put her foot on a clutch shouldn't be allowed on a dance floor.''

''I did?'' he asked, still looking baffled. He pushed the hat back on his head and ran a hand through his hair. ''Let me think here a minute.'' He toed the ground, then shook his head. ''Nope. That's not what I said. I said that a woman who couldn't take direction when it came to using a clutch probably wouldn't let the man lead on the dance floor.''

"And that's *better?*" Ginger demanded, planting her hands on her hips. "Sam Weller, you're not only an opinionated, quarrelsome cowboy—you're a chauvinist, too!"

"You make that sound like a bad thing," he said, his mouth twitching.

"You're damn right it's a bad thing!" she shouted at him.

Sam began laughing, and that flustered Ginger more than his irritating remarks had.

"Now what's so funny?" she demanded.

"Honey, I finally got you to swear," he said, grinning at her, looking totally unrepentant. "Believe me, I have never met a woman as…ladylike as you are."

"Ladylike?" she repeated in disbelief. "Do I look ladylike to you?" She gestured down at her dirty pink shorts, her knees, which were covered with grass stains, and her old tennis shoes, so worn that one pink-polished toe poked through the canvas.

Sam drew in a deep breath. "Yes, ma'am," he said with a growl in his throat. "You'd look ladylike if you were mud wrestling."

She didn't have an answer to that, so she just opened her mouth and closed it again. And felt the blood creep up her face as she suddenly realized he'd called her *honey*.

Sam's lazy grin faded as he slanted his head toward her. Ginger found herself unable to move as his big hands spanned her waist, holding her still as his mouth hovered over hers. A second—or an eternity—later, he was kissing her, his mouth tasting and teasing, coaxing hers into opening in response. And respond she did.

She was suddenly overheated, and from far more than the sun overhead.

Her cap fell to the ground as he tilted her head back, and she clutched at Sam's arms to keep her balance. She made a soft moan against his mouth, and that broke the spell. Abruptly he came back to his senses.

Ginger was still swimming in a cloud of sensuality. The earth was spinning wildly, and she could have sworn she heard a buzzing in her ears. Belatedly she realized that the buzzing was Ratso, snoring on the porch.

"Damn," Sam said softly, holding her away from him. "I don't know why I keep doing that." He saw her cap on the ground just then and bent to pick it up.

"And just why are you wearing a cap that says Older than Dirt?" he asked with a raised brow, trying not to look at that sweet, pretty face, with the bowed lips he had just kissed so thoroughly. He couldn't seem to look at her anymore without picturing her in his bed.

"Actually, I got it for you," she said, crossing her arms and giving him a pert look, deciding to ignore his remark about why he kept kissing her.

"After the lecture you gave me about my not being all that old?"

Ginger shrugged. "I figured you're too darn stubborn to change, so I'm going along with your little delusions."

Sam chuckled. "And you decided to go along with them by getting me this cap?"

"Mm-hmmm." She glanced at the ground and then up at him again, as if what she was going to say next weren't easy. "I can't see your eyes in that cowboy hat."

Sam looked surprised. "And why do you have to see my eyes?"

Ginger frowned. "Because I don't know when you're teasing me and when you're serious if I can't see your eyes."

Sam considered refusing to wear the cap on those grounds alone. He had found that he rather liked teasing her. He even liked the prickly way she challenged him when she felt insulted, the way she had confronted him over the dancing remark.

Sam doffed his cowboy hat and plopped it on Ginger's head before settling the black cap on his head. "I'm not sure this is going to help you see my eyes," he said, smiling lazily at her as he pulled the brim down.

"That's because you're not wearing it right," she told him, reaching up and turning the cap around backward. She had to tilt her head far back to see, since his cowboy hat came down nearly to her nose. "There. That's better."

Sam gave her a wry look. "My mother's going to think I'm listening to rap music and talking about the 'hood if she sees me in this cap."

"How do you do that?" Ginger asked.

"Do what?"

"Make one eyebrow go up and the other go down like that," she said, pretending to study his face. Which wasn't hard to do, since she considered it a pretty nice view. "Are you double-jointed, or ambidextrous, or something like that?"

"You're trying to change the subject," he said accusingly.

"The subject was your face," she retorted.

"No, it wasn't. We were talking about this cap."

"Well, it's your face in that cap."

They were so involved in their verbal sparring that neither of them heard the car approaching until a horn honked.

"Is that—" Ginger began in dismay.

"They're early," Sam muttered, crossing his arms.

Emily came dashing around the house, her hair flying. "Is that Sam's mom?" she asked, coming to a breathless stop beside Ginger.

"Yes, sweetie," Ginger said, smoothing down her shorts in a near panic. She looked a mess! She wished Sam's hat would just sink down to her knees and cover everything.

Jeannie slid out from the driver's side and waved to them before moving behind the car to open the trunk. Sam hurried toward her to help, while Ginger trailed behind.

The woman who got out the passenger side was sort of what Ginger had expected—but much smaller. She couldn't be much taller than five feet, even in those three-inch heels. The memory of Sam's dread of this little woman nearly started Ginger chuckling. This tiny creature, in her dark purple pants suit and layers of jewelry, had driven Sam Weller to rent a fiancée.

"Interesting hats," Enid said, looking from Sam's hat to Ginger's.

"Mother, this is Ginger," Sam said. "And her daughter Emily. I guess Jeannie told you that we're engaged." He shot his sister a significant look over his shoulder.

Enid shook the hand that Ginger held out. "Yes, she did," she said evenly, drawing herself up to her full height, such as it was. "And for the life of me, I can't understand why you wouldn't tell me the good news yourself.''

''Because I was so looking forward to surprising you on your visit,'' Sam said, and Ginger could have sworn that he bared his teeth more than smiled.

''Well,'' Enid said to Ginger, ''at least I do get to meet you, dear. And your lovely daughter.'' She smiled at Emily. ''Knowing Sam, I'm surprised he didn't just invent an imaginary fiancée to keep me from showing up.''

At that, Sam nearly dropped Enid's suitcase. But she was already on her way up the steps, picking her way around Ratso.

''I see you still have the twenty-five-pound door-stop,'' she observed as she glanced down at the dog before opening the door and sweeping inside regally.

''Wow,'' Ginger breathed. ''Isn't she something?''

''Yeah, she's something, all right,'' Sam said beside her.

''And you're scared of her,'' Ginger said, grinning.

''What? Of course I'm not.'' He scowled down at her as she pushed the hat back on her head so that she could see his face.

''Yes, you are,'' she insisted. ''And that's funny, because you're so big and she's such a little thing.''

''I am *not* scared of her,'' he hissed under his breath as she held the screen door for him.

''Oh, yes, he is,'' Jeannie affirmed as she followed him in, winking at Ginger. ''We all are. She's like the Mafia don of motherhood.''

''What's that mean?'' Emily asked her mother, and Ginger ruffled her hair.

''That means I'm going to enjoy this,'' Ginger said, grinning.

* * *

Ginger had run back home to shower and change clothes, putting on cream-colored slacks and a light blue cotton sweater. She had left Emily with Mrs. Turner, whose granddaughter was staying with her. She had to admit to herself that she didn't need the distraction of worrying about what Emily would say to Enid's questions about Sam and Ginger's engagement.

When Ginger walked through the screen door on her return, she could hear Sam still going at it with his mother.

"I don't know why you don't get that dog a hobby," Enid was saying. "He didn't even move a muscle when I nearly stepped on him on the way in."

"That's because he was blinded when the sun hit your necklace," Sam shot back.

"I was not about to pack my jewelry in the suitcase," Enid said. "You never know if it will end up here or halfway around the world." She smiled suddenly when she saw Ginger coming into the kitchen. "My, don't you look nice!" she said. "Sam, I must admit that you've made an excellent choice. Now, come over here, dear, and tell me how you and Sam met."

"Really, Mother, we don't want to embarrass Ginger by prying," Jeannie said, clearing her throat. "Why don't we help her make lunch?"

"You two stay where you are and chat," Ginger said cheerfully. She opened the refrigerator and began to pull out some things to fix lunch. "Actually, it was Jeannie who set us up on a blind date."

"I did," Jeannie said, sounding far from sure about the event in question.

"And when Sam found out how much I like to fish, he brought me out here to his lake," Ginger said.

"And she caught a trophy tuna," Sam interjected dryly.

"Well, not exactly a tuna," Ginger said lightly. "But Sam's a little upset about that fishing trip. Seems I caught four largemouth bass, and he got one tiny sunfish." She smiled at Sam, who looked as if he were swallowing something large. At the table, a sputtering cough came from Jeannie.

"Well," Enid said, looking from one to the other. "I think Sam's finally met his match. Now, Jeannie, when are you and Pete going to make me a grandmother?"

Jeannie groaned, and Enid fished in her purse to pull out a list of herbs that she assured Jeannie would enhance her fertility.

Giving Sam a dazzling smile, Ginger reached into one of the kitchen drawers and pulled out the frilly apron she'd picked up when she bought the bedspreads. Calmly she pulled it over her head. She was fumbling with the ties at the back when Sam stepped up behind her.

"Let me do that," he said, in a barely controlled voice. Bending closer to Ginger, he said softly, "You're enjoying this, aren't you?"

Ginger hid her smile, trying not to laugh as Sam pulled the apron ties together with more force than necessary and tied them tightly. "There you go, Betty Crocker," he teased her, giving her a soft smack on her bottom that neither Jeannie nor Enid, on the other side of the counter, could see. They were still engrossed in an apparently ongoing argument about the production of Jeannie's progeny.

"Now, do you want me to cut up some vegetables or something?" Sam asked.

She looked at him in surprise. "You want to help?"

He cocked an eyebrow at the table. "It's better than listening to Mother lecture on herbal concoctions to boost sperm viability."

Ginger grinned and pointed him toward the refrigerator. "The veggies are already cut up, but you could put them out on a plate."

She watched him from the corner of her eye as he got out the bowl and nudged the refrigerator door shut with his hip. He was still wearing the cap she'd given him, and it made him look more youthful than he did in the cowboy hat. He had on his jeans and a gray sweatshirt he'd pushed up at the elbows. Despite his protestations that he was eager to get his mother off his back and on her way home to Hawaii, Ginger saw only affection in his eyes whenever he looked at Enid. Or at Jeannie, for that matter.

"Now, dear," Enid said when Ginger set large crusty rolls and sliced cheese and ham on the table, "when is the wedding date?" From her purse, she pulled a worn engagement book and began flipping through it. "Christmas would be nice. The church could be decorated with candles and holly."

"I, uh…" Ginger began, faltering as she searched for some excuse—any excuse—for not getting married at Christmas.

"We hate to disappoint you, Mother," Sam put in smoothly, "but Ginger's going to be a June bride."

"*June?*" Enid cried. "But that's so long from now. What if she discovers what a lousy catch you are in the meantime?"

"I'll just have to take that chance," Sam said, smiling, and Ginger was pretty sure he was already planning just such an occurrence once his mother was out of his hair.

Enid sighed. "I suppose that will give me more time to work out the details. What about your parents, Ginger? I'd be glad to take care of the wedding, if they wouldn't mind."

"My parents aren't living," Ginger said, realizing as soon as she said it that she'd just left the door open for Enid to take charge.

Enid rubbed her hands together with gusto. "Well! I'm sorry to hear that, but I can see that my services are needed, then."

"Really, Mother..." Sam began.

But Enid waved away his objections. "Let's get the date pinned down first," she said, slipping on her reading glasses. "Have you reserved the church yet?"

"Well, no..." Ginger said uncomfortably.

"Good gracious, I've got to get right on that!" Enid exclaimed, leaping up to riffle through the phone book. "Church preference?" she asked Ginger, looking over her glasses.

"I'm fairly new in town," Ginger said weakly. "I really don't know any...."

"You just leave it to me, dear," Enid insisted. "I know how to be persuasive with ministers."

"Now there's an understatement," Jeannie muttered, and Ginger remembered Sam's story about Jeannie's wedding. Maybe he hadn't been exaggerating, she thought in sudden panic.

She shot Sam a pleading glance, and he rolled his eyes. "Don't worry," he said in an undertone. "Whatever she does, we can undo again."

Enid was too busy to hear him, insisting into the

phone that it was imperative that she have the church the first Saturday in June. And, no, she didn't care that the youth choir's spring concert was scheduled for that day. In fact, she would be delighted if the concert served as the backdrop for the wedding.

"And then you'd have a guaranteed crowd," she said sweetly into the phone.

"Oh, Lord," Ginger whispered, glancing at Jeannie. *What had she gotten herself into?* "What are we going to do?"

"Don't look at me," Jeannie said with a sigh. "I'm still wondering if I can flush two pounds of herbs and a teakwood fertility goddess down the toilet without ruining the septic system."

"Just go along with her," Sam said quietly. "Nothing's permanent."

"There!" Enid announced triumphantly as she hung up the phone. "The church and the minister are set. Now, what about flowers and the cake? And your china pattern?" She beamed at Ginger and Sam, and both of them smiled wanly back at her.

"I thought I'd do the cake myself," Ginger suggested quickly. "I'm a caterer."

"Wonderful," Enid said, nodding her approval. "I can arrange the flowers later. Once we decide on the bridesmaids' dresses."

Ginger shuddered at the thought of all this futile planning. There would be no wedding. And letting Enid plan an imaginary one was nerve-racking.

"Now," Enid said, enthusiastically biting into her sandwich, "tomorrow Ginger and I will go to St. Louis to pick out the china."

Sam gave an exasperated sigh. "Mother, Ginger

doesn't have time to run around shopping with you. She has a business to run.''

"Well, of course, dear. How thoughtless of me.'' Enid brightened even more, if that was possible. "We'll all go next Saturday.'' She held up her hand as Sam started to object. "I'm not listening, son. Someone has to take charge of this wedding, and, lucky for you, I'm available.''

"I just hope I don't get any luckier,'' Sam muttered under his breath.

"Lovely lunch,'' Enid complimented Ginger. "I can see you're a wonderful caterer.''

Ginger tried to smile. For a moment, she actually envied Ratso, snoozing on the porch. At least Enid wasn't meddling in his life.

It was early evening when Ginger ventured out onto the front porch with her box of fudge and sat on the top step, stretching out her legs and sighing. She had gone back to Rent-a-Wife after lunch, working there until dinnertime. Now, the evening meal was done, the dishes were in the dishwasher, and Sam and the rest of his family were in the back room off the kitchen, watching a comedy about outer space aliens on the television.

Jeannie had brought Pete back for dinner, and Ginger had brought Emily, who seemed delighted by the extended family that now surrounded her.

Ginger gave an appreciative glance upward at the stars before using the plastic knife to cut off a sliver of the fudge and slide it into her mouth.

"I used to bring a martini out here,'' an amused voice said behind her, nearly startling her into dropping the fudge. "Maybe I should have tried chocolate instead."

Ginger turned her head and saw Enid sitting in the wicker chair in the darkness of the porch. Ginger had cleaned the chair and made a pillow for it just two days before.

"I thought you were inside with the others, watching the show," Ginger said hesitantly, wondering whether her presence was an intrusion.

"I can take aliens or leave them," Enid said, smiling, her hand patting Ratso, on her lap. She glanced down at the dog. "I just can't seem to break this guy from jumping up on my lap."

Ginger smiled herself, since they both knew how much of a lie that was. She held out the fudge box, and Enid murmured her thanks as she sliced off a piece.

"You're going to need a lot of this if you marry my son," Enid said, eyeing Ginger speculatively. She sighed. "But I imagine you can afford the calories. You're one of those little dynamos who burns food faster than you can eat it. My personal theory is that girls like you have a secret gene that can't store fat. I'm going in for an implant as soon as it's discovered."

Ginger laughed, but she chose to focus on Enid's comment about Sam.

"Was Sam a difficult little boy?" she asked.

Enid shook her head, licking the fudge from her fingers. "He was just like his father. This land is his whole world. Sam's father never went past his front gate. It was like his feet were rooted in the dirt."

"It's not a bad place to be rooted," Ginger said mildly. In truth, she found the peacefulness of the place like a balm to her soul.

Enid shrugged. "No Neiman Marcus. No Red Lobster restaurants. No Broadway theaters.'' She stroked Ratso's ears.

''A person can always take a vacation,'' Ginger suggested.

''That was my problem. I wanted a permanent vacation. I wanted to go to those places all the time. It's like that fudge.'' She leaned over and sliced off another piece. ''One taste is too much, and a hundred tastes not enough.''

Ginger felt a rush of sympathy for Enid. It must have been hard on her, wanting things that couldn't be had on the ranch. And yet, she had loved her husband and son. She must have felt torn in two.

''Sam's father was a kind man, and he said he understood.'' Her voice was wistful and low. ''And after seeing what happened to me and to Denise, Sam believed that no woman would stay with him. I certainly set a poor example, and I blame only myself.''

''Sam understands,'' Ginger said. ''He doesn't blame you.'' But even as she said the words, she wasn't sure they were true. As far as she knew, Sam blamed all womankind for the inconstancy of the women he'd known best.

''Well, I'm just glad he's found you,'' Enid said. She paused. ''Now, if I could just get Jeannie started on that grandchild.''

Ginger laughed. ''Here,'' she said, handing Enid the box of fudge. ''Some of my best ideas came while I was eating chocolate.''

7

The next three nights, Ginger arrived at Sam's house with Emily in time to cook dinner. After they all ate together, Ginger loaded the dishwasher with Sam's help before going home. Sam had tried to coax her into staying longer, but she had come up with a handy excuse for leaving early each time.

She knew that Sam was paying her for this, and it was to her advantage to stay there the extra hours, but she was feeling more unsettled about this arrangement. She didn't quite understand why, but it bothered her to have Enid accepting her so readily as her future daughter-in-law. Since Monday night on the porch, Enid had treated her almost like some kind of coconspirator in a get-Sam-to-the-altar scheme. Whenever Sam complimented her dinner—which was every night—or paused while they loaded the dishwasher to rub her shoulder, Enid would wink at Ginger and smile.

So Ginger resolved to spend as little time at the ranch as possible. Friday night, she planned to leave right after dinner again, pleading tiredness. But as soon as she walked through the door, she saw that her excuse wasn't going to work.

Water covered the kitchen floor, and a flustered Enid was frantically trying to mop it up with paper towels while the dishwasher spewed even more sudsy water on top of the deluge.

"Oh, thank heavens you're here!" Enid cried. "Sam's coming back from the pasture any minute now, and I can't get this infernal thing to stop flooding the kitchen."

Ginger quickly took charge, sending Emily to the closet for the mop while she kicked off her shoes and waded through the water to turn off the dishwasher. She was in the backyard, wringing out the mop, when Sam rounded the corner from the pasture, his baseball cap firmly in place. When he saw the mop, he groaned.

"She didn't try to cook, did she?" he asked in a low voice.

Ginger shook her head. "She was running the dishwasher, and a hose broke."

"She's driving me crazy, Ginger," Sam said, shoving the cap back on his head. "She's at loose ends, and I can't keep her entertained. Can't you stay around here longer?"

Ginger sighed. It was the first time she'd heard even a hint of pleading in his voice, and she knew he must be at the end of his rope to ask this of her. She dared a look into his eyes and saw a tenderness there that she guessed was for his mother. No matter how aggravating Enid might be, she was still family.

"All right," she said. "Let me get this cleaned up, and I'll fix dinner, then play cards with her or something."

She turned to go back in, but Sam's hand on her arm stopped her.

Sam shook his head. "Dinner's on me tonight. You've been holding up your end of the bargain all week. Now it's my turn."

"I don't know." She couldn't seem to stop looking into his eyes, which was a big mistake. At that moment, she might have said yes to anything. "I mean, I really should..."

Her voice trailed off, and Sam smiled slowly. "You seem to be having a hard time agreeing to a simple dinner out. It's not like I'm asking you to sit on my lap during the meal, or anything like that. It's just dinner out, Ginger."

Now she was beginning to flush at the thought of sitting on his lap. She couldn't think straight when he was touching her, and she finally made herself pull her arm away and nod her head.

"Fine." She backed away from him, wondering why an invitation to dinner out with his mother and her daughter would leave her so addled.

It was her loss of control over the whole evening, she realized as she hurried back to the kitchen. As long as she came to the ranch and did her work here, she felt a modicum of control. But this was Sam's night now. And Ginger braced herself to go along with his plans.

He followed her into the kitchen, where they found Emily faithfully dabbing at the water with a paper towel, while Enid sat on the counter with wide eyes.

"The water's rising," she said, to no one in particular.

"No, it's not," Ginger reassured her. "I turned off the dishwasher. We'll just get this mopped up, and everything will be fine."

"And, if not, I'll get out the ark," Sam teased Enid.

Ginger turned to give him a pert look, and when she did, her right foot went sliding out from under her and she gave a little squeak as she started to fall. But Sam was there instantly, catching her around her waist and pulling her to him.

His hands lingered far longer than necessary, but Ginger couldn't seem to make herself pull away. She forgot all about Enid as her bones began to go mushy on her. Another minute of him touching her, and she would dissolve right down into the pool of water at her feet.

It was Enid who finally broke the spell.

"Was that thunder, or my stomach growling?" she asked.

"Are you trying to tell us you're hungry, Mother?" Sam asked, still not taking his eyes off Ginger. "I thought I saw you eating some fudge just an hour ago."

"Well, yes," Enid admitted. "But that wasn't for sustenance. That was more in the line of a tranquilizer. You know how I am around cattle."

"You were around the cattle?" Sam asked incredulously, finally turning to give her his full attention.

"I saw some mint growing by the fence," she said defensively, "and you know that's such a good aphrodisiac." She took a deep breath and wrinkled her brow. "Although, now that I think about it, it might not be mint I want. Maybe it was thyme."

"Mother," Sam said in a strained voice, "what on earth are you doing scouring the earth for aphrodisiacs?"

Enid hopped off the counter and faced him, drawing herself up to her full height. She was about as imposing as a sparrow.

"It's just that you and Ginger don't seem very... physical. Well, at least not until this moment. I mean, I was thinking that I'm cramping your style where your love life is concerned, and I was looking for something that might work for you.''

"Oh, you're cramping my style, all right," he told her grimly. "But Ginger and I can handle it just fine. Don't worry."

"All right," Enid said brightly.

"Now let's get ready for dinner. I'm taking us all out tonight."

Enid dusted off her hands. "Fine with me. And, son?"

"What is it, Mother?"

"Why don't you order the oysters?" she suggested, her eyes sparkling. "They might jump start your libido."

Sam was caught by a sudden coughing fit, and Ginger felt herself blushing even more.

Emily, who had been listening avidly, looked from one adult to the other.

"What's a lee-bee-do?" she asked, puzzled.

Sam and Ginger looked at each other, and Ginger felt herself blushing all over again.

"My muscles," Sam said finally, in a choked voice. "Mother believes an old superstition that says oysters make a person...strong." He looked at Ginger again, but she couldn't meet his eyes. She didn't know whose neck to wring first, Sam's or Enid's. And Enid just stood there smiling serenely.

"Well, are we going to eat, or are we going to stand here debating the merits of aphrodisiacs?" Enid chirped brightly.

"I'll explain later," Ginger said quickly to Emily, who looked on the verge of asking another question. Much later, Ginger added to herself. Like in ten years or so.

Sam held the front door for them, advising them to watch out for Ratso, who was sprawled on the edge of the porch, right at the top of the steps.

"I'm beginning to think you put Valium in his dog food," Enid observed as she gingerly skirted a silky ear.

"Now there's an idea," Sam said darkly.

"Sam, the dog's tranquil enough," Enid complained.

"Not for him, Mother. For you."

Sam drove them to the Barge, a floating restaurant on the small bay. The base of the place actually was a barge, but small brick walls had been erected around the edge, with ivy growing over them. Half of the restaurant was glassed and roofed in, but the other half, where Sam had them seated, was out in the open, with a beautiful view of the water around them and the open sky above. The sun was setting, and streetlights winked on along the riverfront, their reflection sparkling like diamonds on the inky water.

"It's a boat!" Emily exclaimed, nearly jumping up and down in her excitement.

"Indeed it is," Enid said with dismay. "Maybe I should get a table that's a little more...landlocked. You know how I get on things that move."

"The boat isn't going anywhere, Mother," Sam assured her. "You'll be fine."

The hostess seated them, and Ginger gave a quiet, involuntary groan when their waitress appeared. She was Marilou, Mrs. Turner's daughter and the mother of Emily's favorite playmate.

"Well, look who's here," Marilou said, smiling brightly at them as she set down the glasses of water.

Sam introduced his mother, and Marilou beamed at her and asked if she was going to be staying for a while.

"Only until I get the wedding plans made," Enid answered promptly, causing Ginger's stomach to sink to her toes.

Marilou looked from Sam to Ginger in surprise, and Enid immediately filled her in, prompting Ginger to show Marilou her engagement ring.

"They've decided on a June wedding," Enid said. "Though why my son would wait that long to make it legal is a mystery to me."

"My goodness," Marilou said. "Wait until my mother hears about this."

Ginger sighed inwardly. Half the town came by Mrs. Turner's fudge shop at least once a week. Enid might as well have announced the engagement on Main Street at high noon.

Sam leaned over to whisper loudly to Ginger, "Do you want to throw her overboard, or shall I?"

Ginger couldn't help but smile.

"What are you two whispering about?" Enid demanded, with a smile of her own. "You aren't planning on eloping and cheating me out of this wedding, are you? If you go off to her house in the middle of the night and carry her and her suitcase down a ladder, I swear I'll move in with the two of you until the first child is born. And maybe after that, too."

"We wouldn't think of it, Mother," Sam assured her. "Besides, my muscles are too weak from hunger right now to carry anything heavier than a steak."

It had been a valiant attempt on Sam's part to turn the conversation back to the menu, but it didn't work.

Emily chose that particular moment to put in her two cents' worth.

"If your muscles are weak, you should eat oysters," she informed him. "They're good for your lee-bee-do."

Marilou's eyes widened for a moment, and then she burst out laughing. Ginger wanted to crawl under the table, and even Enid looked taken aback before a mischievous smile lit her eyes.

"Just what I need," Sam muttered good-naturedly. "Another female worried about my libido." But he reached across the table to ruffle Emily's hair, and she grinned back at him.

Marilou left them then, and Ginger covertly studied Sam as he studied the menu. She almost missed the question Enid just asked.

"How long have you and Sam known each other now?"

Emily piped up. "Since Saturday."

"Yes, it was a Saturday when we went fishing," Ginger added quickly. "A memorable Saturday."

"I'll never forget the tuna she caught," Sam threw in, with a teasing glance in her direction.

"It was several catfish," Ginger corrected him. "At least five."

"I thought they were largemouth bass," Enid said hesitantly, and Ginger felt a moment of panic.

"Largemouth bass and catfish," Ginger confirmed. "Three of one and two of the other." She could feel a sheen of perspiration forming above her lip. She had never known that lying could take such a physical toll. She was actually suffering the beginnings of an upset stomach, as well.

"She may not know their names, but she sure can

catch them," Sam said. "Maybe I should have her take you fishing while you're here, Mother."

Ginger kicked him under the table, and he squeezed her hand, grinning.

Enid held up her hands. "Not me, thank you. I don't like live fish any better than live cows." She pointed at the menu. "Prime rib. Now that's how I like my cows."

Sam leaned back and listened to his mother discussing her various animal aversions. Normally, her conversation made him restless and edgy, anxious to be anyplace but where he was. But tonight was different. And he realized that it was Ginger who made his mother so tolerable.

He had actually had to stop himself from laughing out loud when Ginger started elaborating on the fish she'd supposedly caught. It had been years since he enjoyed himself as much as he was tonight.

Don't get used to it, he reminded himself. As soon as his mother was airborne for Hawaii, he and Ginger would go back to their separate lives. It was how he wanted it. It was just what he'd planned.

Midway through their dinner, Enid caught Ginger off guard again when she asked a question about where she'd lived before coming to London, Missouri.

"I believe Jeannie said you and Emily are from St. Louis. Is that right?"

Ginger swallowed a bite of her fish and nodded. "I grew up there."

"Really?" Enid said, looking puzzled. "Why on earth would you leave the city, then?"

"The usual reasons," Ginger said with a smile. "I wanted to get away from the hustle and bustle."

Enid looked even more surprised. "But why?"

"Believe me, Mother," Sam drawled. "Not everybody worships high-rise apartments and concrete."

"I suppose cow manure and hay fever have their charms," Enid retorted before turning her attention back to Ginger. "Was your late husband from there, dear?"

Clay. The heated argument she had had with Sam in his bedroom about her marriage leaped into her mind. And, with a growing sense of unease, she realized that for some reason she couldn't seem to summon Clay's face to her mind.

"Yes, he was," Ginger said, toying with her baked potato. "His cousins still live in St. Louis."

"Well, it must have taken a lot of fortitude for you to uproot yourself and come all the way here," Enid said, gesturing around herself delicately, as if pointing out a third-world country.

"Oh, Emily and I like it here," Ginger assured her. "There's nothing like the warmth of a small town."

As if to confirm her sentiment, Marilou appeared at that moment, bearing a small cake topped with a lighted candle.

"I'm sorry, but this is the only song we know," she said, and she and the three waitresses with her began singing, "Happy engagement to you," to the tune of "Happy Birthday."

Ginger smiled through the rendition and gamely blew out the candle when they were done, but a troubling development had settled in her brain and refused to leave. Clay's face had faded away in her memory, and the one that had replaced it was Sam's.

* * *

"I *cannot* eat all this food you and Ginger are putting into me," Enid complained, without conviction, as they left the restaurant.

"Nobody's holding a fork to your head," Sam teased her mildly. He had idly taken Ginger's hand in his, making her pulse race, despite their leisurely walking speed.

"It's just that Ginger is such a darn good cook, and this restaurant out here in the middle of Podunk, North America, actually has decent cuisine. I'm going to burst if this keeps up."

Warmed by the compliment, Ginger assured Enid that she would fix her a salad for dinner the next day. And Sam suggested that they all take a walk along the river to burn off a few of the calories. As they headed toward the city park, they could hear the soft strains of music drifting to them from the pavilion.

"I forgot," Sam said. "It's Friday night. The city band always plays."

"It sounds like a polka," Enid said, sighing in disappointment. "Do you think the band knows any samba music?"

Sam laughed. "The city band consists of three dentists and a retired proctologist," he told her. "You might get a waltz out of them, but nothing flashy."

Emily piped up hopefully. "I like dancing."

"Then I'll have to ask you for the first dance," Sam said with a smile.

And that was just what he did, settling Enid and Ginger on a park bench near the river as he led Emily out in front of the bandstand. A waltz was winding down, and the band picked up the tempo with another polka. Ginger watched in amusement, expecting Sam to more or less hop around in place with Emily. But, to her surprise, he actually knew how to polka. To her further surprise, he looked darn good doing it. For a big man, he was very light on his feet. His movements were somewhat hampered by having to bend at the waist to accommodate Emily, but still he managed to look fluid and athletic at the same time.

Emily was grinning from ear to ear when they returned at the end of the polka. The band members consulted for a moment, studying their music sheets over bifocals, then began a slow fox-trot.

Enid snapped her fingers. "I totally forgot. We have to plan your honeymoon."

"Sorry, Mother," Sam said quickly, "but I'm going to dance with my bride-to-be."

"Me?" Ginger stared at him in surprise.

"I don't see any other potential brides standing around," he said, making a show of looking behind her.

"But I thought I was the woman who shouldn't be allowed on a dance floor because she couldn't keep her left foot on the clutch."

"I was wrong," he said with a half smile.

"So, I'm not such a bad driver with a stick shift?"

"I didn't say that," he retorted, his eyes devilish. "Now, come here, and let's see what kind of dancer you are."

Not wanting to take a chance on sinking her heeled sandals into the soft grass, Ginger kicked them off and let him lead her barefoot toward the pavilion. The music washed over her like the night breeze, and she gave an involuntary shiver as Sam's hand tightened on her own.

Moonlight and the muted glow of street lamps

glazed the pavilion and its surroundings, turning the dewy grass into a carpet of silver. Ginger's bare toes curled into the dampness just as her hand curled into Sam's shoulder.

It was dangerous to let him hold her like this, she thought as he drew her into his arms and began to move to the music. She could feel his hard thigh as it brushed her leg when they moved, and his hand at her back was positively unnerving. His fingers pressed her gently, but they seemed to have a direct link to her nerve endings. She tingled all over.

He was a *cowboy,* she told herself. He was grumpy and rude and irritating.

But he made her pulse leap. And he could be very tender when he wanted to be. Both of which made it imprudent for her to be in his arms like this.

She made a soft sound in her throat, and Sam pulled her closer, cradling her head against his chest. She could hear the steady beat of his heart, and it soothed her.

"We have to tell her something," he whispered, and at first she didn't understand. "Mother will be making reservations at the Honolulu Hilton for us unless we derail her."

The honeymoon. *The nonexistent honeymoon,* she reminded herself. They had to come up with another lie.

"You know," she groused, "I never knew that trying to fool someone could be so exhausting. Do you suppose criminals get worn out with all the mental effort?"

Sam laughed softly. "I don't think it's work for them, honey. Now, how about we tell Mother that we're going to stay right here in London after the wedding and spend some time on the river? We'll say we're going to rent a houseboat.''

"Your mother won't let a plan like that alone for a minute," she said immediately.

"It's just something to tell her. Don't worry about it.''

"But, Sam—"

"I'll take care of it. Don't worry."

He was being high-handed and stubborn again, insisting on handling this himself, and she glared up at him. To her surprise, he dipped his head and kissed her, taking the starch out of her irritation.

"That wasn't fair," she muttered, when he finally raised his head and she could breathe again. Her heart was thudding against her ribs.

"Maybe not," he said softly, "but it seems to be the only way I can get around you.''

She opened her mouth to give him a sassy reply, but he turned and tugged her toward Enid and Emily. She realized belatedly that the music had ended.

Enid was smiling happily at the two of them. She handed Ginger her sandals and resumed her conversation as if the five-minute interval of the dance had never interrupted them.

"I was thinking that you two should come to Hawaii for your honeymoon. I can get you booked anywhere you want. I have friends at every hotel. We all play bridge together.''

"Ah…" Sam said. "I'm sorry to disappoint you, Mother, but Ginger and I are going to rent a houseboat and stay on the river.''

Enid looked at him, aghast, as if he had suggested that they were going to check into the Bates Motel and shower together.

"The *river?*" she demanded. Then she relaxed a bit.

"Oh, you must mean the Amazon, right? Or maybe the Nile? That is what you mean, isn't it?"

"The Mississippi, Mother," Sam said, looking as if he were just realizing that he had made a mistake in judgment.

"Oh, no. No, no." Enid shook her head vigorously. "No way. If it's water you want, water you'll get. But not this big drink of mud. No, I'm making reservations for you on a cruise. That's it. A cruise to South America. A three-week cruise. Now, that's a honeymoon."

"Mother, I can't leave the ranch for three weeks. It's impossible."

"We'll take the cows to the kennel," Enid said decisively.

Poor Sam looked as if he had just come to the end of a short rope. Ginger almost felt sorry for him. Almost.

"Cattle are not like dogs, Mother," he said through gritted teeth. "You don't kennel them."

Enid waved away his objections with a ring-bedecked hand. Ginger realized it was time for her to step in before she ended up on a cruise with a man she had no intention of marrying—or vice versa, for that matter.

"Oh, Enid, that's so thoughtful of you," Ginger said sweetly, "but, actually, I've got a little surprise for Sam."

Sam looked at her suspiciously, and she smiled blandly at him. "I've already booked us into the most wonderful spa in California. I was waiting for the right moment to surprise Sam."

"A spa," Enid said. "Now that sounds relaxing."

"Oh, it is," Ginger said, slipping her feet into her sandals. "It's totally vegetarian. Sam's going to love their tofu surprise. And the classes in yoga."

Sam seemed to be trying not to choke.

Enid linked her arm with Ginger's and started back toward the truck. "Oh, I bet they give pedicures and everything there."

"I've signed up Sam for a mud pack and a cucumber facial," Ginger confided.

Enid laughed. "Ginger, you are far and away the best medicine for my son. I say this as a totally biased future mother-in-law. My dear, welcome to the family." She threw her head back and laughed.

Ginger tried not to glance at Sam, who was now walking beside her, holding Emily's hand, but she couldn't resist. What she saw set her heart thumping all over again.

"Tofu surprise," he muttered softly.

And when Ginger saw the amused look in his eyes, she knew that he had more than her fabricated honeymoon on his mind.

Sam didn't say a word as he drove Ginger and Emily to their home. From the back seat of the extended cab, Enid chattered endlessly about what a delight spas were, and how she was going to have to book herself into one sometime this year. Ginger half listened and made sympathetic noises, but all she could think of was the man beside her, and the way she still tingled all over, just thinking about how he had held her dancing.

Sam parked a couple of stores down from Ginger's shop, and thankfully, the streetlight didn't illuminate the Rent-a-Wife lettering on the green awning. Ginger scooted out of the truck before Sam could come around to open the door for her. She reached into the back and helped a giggling Emily climb down. Waving goodnight to Enid, Ginger started toward the shop, with Emily beside her.

"Wait a minute." His voice stopped her in her

tracks, and she slowly turned to him. "I forgot to give you this earlier," Sam said, but he was looking at Emily and not Ginger.

Sam reached into the back of the truck bed and held up a round rock and a chisel and hammer. Kneeling on the sidewalk, he held the chisel against the rock and began to tap it with the hammer, first in one place, then another, until he had made a circle around the middle of the rock.

"What is it, Sam?" Emily asked, kneeling beside him.

"A surprise, Em. Now watch." He tapped harder on the rock, then gave it one final blow. It split in two beneath his hands, and he held one of the halves up to the light.

Emily gasped. "It's diamonds!"

Sam laughed gently. "Not quite. It's called a geode. These are crystals inside. I picked it up in the creek when I was checking cattle. Here. This is for you." He handed her the geode, and Emily stared down at it, entranced.

"It's beautiful," she breathed.

"Come on," Sam said. "Let's get you home now. You're almost asleep on your feet."

Emily hurried ahead toward their door, clutching her geode, and Ginger started to follow. She was stopped by Sam's hand closing on her wrist. He turned her to him and immediately drew her close.

"What am I going to do with you?" he murmured huskily, and she could see the light of amusement in his eyes again. Suddenly she was regretting the whole spa honeymoon she'd spun out of thin air for Enid's benefit. She had wanted to get a rise out of Sam. She had to admit that she had enjoyed that look of bemusement on his face. But now...

She cleared her throat nervously. "I should get Emily to bed."

"No, you don't," he whispered. "You're not getting out of this one. You know you've got this coming."

She couldn't imagine what he was going to do here on the sidewalk, while his mother observed from the truck, but her heart had suddenly sped up. She was frozen in front of him, as if her feet were rooted in the ground.

Sam's mouth quirked up at one corner as he pulled her even closer. *"Tofu,"* he muttered just before his mouth came down on hers. He kissed her thoroughly, so thoroughly that she wasn't sure her toes were still on the ground. His tongue teased her lower lip until she groaned against his mouth, and then that seductive tongue slipped inside and played havoc with her senses. Her head was swimming when he finally pulled back and looked down at her. Even in the dim light, she could see the smoky haze in his eyes.

"I think maybe I got more than I bargained for, honey, when I hooked up with you, but that's all right." His smile made her shiver. "Mother's going to enjoy the fireworks."

Ginger didn't know exactly what he meant, but the challenge in his tone made her shiver all over again. She turned to go, but he stopped her once more. Pressing the second half of the geode into her hand, he touched her lips briefly with one finger, then went back to the truck.

Ginger's knees were shaking.

She had the sinking feeling that she had just challenged the top gunslinger in town.

And this cowboy didn't play by the rules.

8

Ginger had anticipated Sam's early arrival the next morning, and she was up and dressed in cream-colored slacks and a soft dark blue cotton sweater, the sleeves pushed up to her elbows.

She had stood in front of the bathroom mirror for ten minutes debating the folly of trying to make herself more presentable for Sam before she caved in to vanity and applied mascara and lipstick. When Emily poked her head inside and asked her what she was doing, Ginger had said her eyes were tired, so she was perking them up. She was beginning to think she was a born liar.

Sam's eyes drifted down her outfit when she answered the door, his eyes lingering momentarily on the soft swell of her breasts. She began to tingle there—and other places, as well—and she abruptly remembered what he'd said the night before: *What am I going to do with you?* Well, she had a couple of ideas about that, but she was interested to see what he would come up with on his own.

"Do you want some coffee?" she offered, trying not to stare at his tight jeans and blue-and-green plaid flannel shirt. "Emily isn't quite ready yet."

He nodded and followed her inside.

"Smells great," he said appreciatively, sniffing in the direction of the skillet filled with eggs and potatoes she had left warming on the stove for Emily.

"Haven't you had any breakfast?"

Sam gave her a significant look. "Do you forget who's staying with me? My mother fixed breakfast this morning before I could beat her to the stove." He gave a heartfelt sigh. "She found the cottage cheese you had in the refrigerator, and she fixed that, with nuts and raisins on top. She heated it, Ginger. Hot cottage cheese for breakfast." He fixed her with a teasingly woeful gaze. "It's all because of that tofu remark you made, you know. So you really owe me a breakfast."

Ginger hid her smile. "Sit down, and I'll see what I can do."

Emily came running into the kitchen, smiling broadly when she saw Sam. "Hi, Sam! You bring me any rocks today?"

"Emily," Ginger said, "you should be thanking him for the one he gave you, not asking for another."

"Thanks, Sam," Emily said, slightly chastened, but still smiling. "I've got it right next to my bed."

Ginger put Emily's breakfast on the table and set about fixing the same for Sam. She listened to Emily chattering about her doll collection and her crayons, and she thought about her own geode, sitting on the table by her bed.

She had fallen asleep the night before, only to wake a couple of hours later, after an X-rated dream about Sam. She had turned over and picked up the rock, tracing her finger over the bumpy crystals inside. The dream had been so erotic that she could still feel heat all over her body. She was a little young yet for hot flashes, so she attributed her physical state to Sam.

She had rested her head on the pillow, smiling as she thought of the tender light in his eyes when he danced with Emily, and the laughter when she teased him.

Lord, she loved that man.

She had sat straight up in bed as the realization hit her. It wasn't possible, she'd told herself. A down-to-earth, commonsense woman like Ginger Marsh didn't fall in love in one week. But, even as she denied it to herself, she'd known deep down that it was true. It was more than a purely physical reaction. She loved his touch, but she loved his ornery, stubborn, gentle soul, as well.

She had thrown in her lot with him. Heck, she had even lied to his mother for him.

Ginger had finally fallen back to sleep, troubled, clutching the geode to her chest.

Now she stole a glance at him over her shoulder and found him studying her. He immediately dropped his eyes, but still she felt shivers slide down her spine. Surely he hadn't guessed what was going through her head. God, she would die if he ever found out she'd fallen in love with him.

Ginger didn't meet his eyes as she set the plate in front of him and sat down across the table with her own coffee.

"Mom makes the best potatoes, doesn't she, Sam?" Emily asked enthusiastically.

"She sure does," Sam said lazily, his eyes drifting over Ginger again, and she knew he wasn't thinking about potatoes at the moment. That knowledge made her flush.

"She makes me potatoes and bacon all the time," Emily informed him.

"She does, huh? No tofu?"

Emily giggled. "Huh-uh. What's tofu?"

"It's the devil's own torture," Sam told her seriously. "And your mother has threatened me with it. Do you know what I'm going to do about that?"

Emily regarded him with wide eyes and avid interest. She shook her head.

He leaned close. "What I'm going to do is—" He abruptly shot a devilish look across the table. "No, that would ruin the surprise."

Ginger couldn't believe that she was actually squirming in her seat. It was just that he was so big and so teasing that he took her breath away.

"Come on, Sam!" Emily cried. "Tell me!"

"Nope," he said, sitting back in his chair. "You'll both just have to wait and see."

Emily's curiosity was diverted when Sam began asking her whether she had ever tried bubble-gum ice cream before. She wrinkled her nose, forgetting all about Sam's teasing threat to her mother as he extolled the gustatory qualities of bubble-gum ice cream and promised to get her a scoop at the ice cream shop before he drove them back to the ranch.

He deliberately looked at Ginger then, no doubt expecting her to express her horror at ice cream in the morning once again. But if he thought she was going to get herself in any deeper at the moment, he was wrong.

Ginger gave him a shaky smile and drank her coffee.

"We have to pick out your china pattern," Enid announced the moment they walked in the door at the ranch, Sam, Ginger and Emily stepping high to clear the snoozing Ratso.

"I really don't think we'd use china very much,"
Ginger said, trying to be tactful. "I can pick out some
stoneware another time."

But Enid was insistent. They were going to St. Louis
to buy china, and that was that. She had them all herded
to the truck before Ginger could set down her purse.

For his part, Sam kept his mouth shut. It wasn't exactly because he was giving in to his mother. He had
to admit that his primary motivation was to get Ginger
off somewhere by herself while his mother entertained
Emily. He rather liked getting her alone and teasing
her, especially since she gave as good as she got. He
nearly chuckled aloud, thinking about the elaborate
tales she'd spun for his mother about their wedding and
honeymoon plans.

Then he sobered as he reminded himself that there
was no wedding in the future. There would be nothing
but a paycheck when Enid left the ranch.

For some reason, that thought dampened his mood,
and he trailed Enid, Emily and Ginger without interest
as his mother led them on the great china expedition.

They started at a jewelry store, but Enid wasn't satisfied with the selection of patterns. So they went on
to another jewelry store, and then a department store.

When they approached the fifth stop, Ginger dropped
back to whisper to Sam, "I'm pretending to fall in love
with the first pattern I see. I don't care if it has a skull
and crossbones on it."

He gave her a mirthless smile, and she frowned up
at him.

"What's wrong? You've been quiet the whole trip."

"Nothing. I'm just not crazy about shopping."

Apparently, she believed that excuse. "We'll wrap
this up," she promised him, putting her hand on his

arm. Immediately he felt the familiar warmth in his groin that her nearness always caused. His little Betty Crocker was one sexy lady. And she was being such a good sport about everything that he decided to give her a little devilment.

He nudged her with his elbow. "Tell Mother you've decided to use paper plates after we're married," he told her.

"Are you nuts?" she demanded. "Do you want to see her have a stroke, right smack in the middle of St. Louis?"

He tamped down his grin. "I want to see what she says."

"*You* tell her," she retorted. "I refuse to be the cause of her total collapse."

They bantered on that way until they reached the housewares department, on the second floor. By then, Sam was openly grinning.

Enid strolled purposefully past the china racks, scrutinizing each one like Captain Ahab checking whales. Ginger tarried behind her, looking around.

"Oh!" Ginger exclaimed suddenly. "Oh, I *love* these!"

She wasn't at the china rack, Sam noticed. Instead, she had picked up a heavy white plate in the stoneware section. It had octagonal sides with raised circles, and in the center of each plate was a sunflower painted in a cheerful country style.

Sam waited for his mother's reaction.

"Oh," Enid said doubtfully, "it does have a certain rustic charm. But...it's *stoneware*, Ginger."

"Well," Ginger said slowly, "Sam was looking at another set over there. The pigs on them have the cutest little snouts."

Enid shuddered. "Oh, no," she said hastily. "I think these plates are just fine."

Emily bounced up and down beside her. "I *love* them! I can have my eggs and potatoes on them every morning."

Sam didn't remember any set with pigs on it, but he hid his smile. Any woman who could get around his mother deserved a medal. His admiration grew.

Ginger pulled him aside as his mother headed for the cash register with her credit card.

"Sam," she whispered urgently, "I can't let her buy those dishes. You'd have to return them after we...well, after there's no wedding."

"Don't worry," he assured her. "You can have the plates. You do like them, don't you?"

"I love them. But that's not the point. It's not fair to make her buy something that won't get used."

Sam placed one finger on her lips to stem her indignant outburst. "We'll share the plates, then, okay?"

"Share them?"

"You get them one weekend, and I get them the next." He smiled down at her. "After all, I have to put my tofu on something."

Ginger gave a rueful smile. "You just aren't going to let go of that tofu remark, are you?"

"No, ma'am," he assured her. "I'm definitely not."

His smile made her warm all over. She couldn't believe she had thought him a cold and stubborn man. Oh, he might still be stubborn, but certainly not in a way that bothered her.

Enid was approaching them, dusting her hands. "They'll have the set all boxed when we're ready to leave the store," she said with satisfaction. "Now, I could use a little pick-me-up. Say, some hot tea and a piece of pie. What about you, Emily? Are you ready for a snack?''

''I'm starved,'' Emily said immediately, and Ginger laughed.

''What about you two?'' Enid asked, turning to Sam and Ginger.

''I think I'll pass on the pie,'' Sam said, and his mother frowned at his uncharacteristic lack of appetite.

''What's going on here?'' she demanded. ''Don't tell me you've converted him to health food, Ginger?''

Ginger couldn't resist the opportunity to tease him a bit.

''Oh, he's hooked on watercress sandwiches now,'' she assured Enid. ''And just the other day he ordered a double café latte with a smattering of whipped cream.''

''You don't say,'' Enid said skeptically.

Sam moved toward Ginger with mock menace. ''Now, woman,'' he said, ''you're going to find out what I'm going to do every time you give me a hard time.''

Ginger swallowed hard, even though she couldn't imagine Sam doing anything too awful. She backed up and found her legs stopped by a table laden with thick towels.

''Now, Sam...'' she said hesitantly.

''Don't you 'Now, Sam' me, honey,'' he told her in a slow drawl. ''You know you've got this coming.''

Her eyes widened as he loomed over her, and she reached behind her, only to find her fists stuffed with towels. What on earth was he planning to do here in the middle of a busy department store?

''People are watching,'' she said in desperation.

''Good,'' he said with satisfaction. He reached out

and tilted up her chin, then gave her a lazy smile just before his mouth lowered to hers.

Oh, my, Ginger thought as her senses swam.

The kiss was long and thorough and so intense that the clerks stopped ringing up sales to stare. Sam's eyes were smoky when he finally lifted his head. One aisle away, a cash register gave a loud ping as its drawer popped open, but for all Ginger knew, the sound was her libido, stretched to its breaking point. .

Enid sighed behind them.

"Ah, love..."

Emily giggled. "Is that what you meant when you said you were going to do something to Mom?" she asked.

"That's it, Em," Sam told her. Ginger saw the mischievous light in his eyes as he looked at her. "Every time your mama gives me trouble, I'm just going to have to kiss her silly."

Oh, my, Ginger thought again.

"Well, are you two coming with us for pie or not?" Enid demanded.

"You and Emily go on, Mother," Sam said. "Meet us back here when you're done. Ginger and I are going to do some more browsing."

"Well, just be careful while you're *browsing,*" she told them saucily. "I don't want to have to bail the two of you out of jail."

Ginger felt warm all over as Sam took her arm and led her toward the other end of the store.

"Where are we going?" she asked, a little wary after that kiss.

"To the book section," he said.

Ginger balked. "I don't know if I'm going anywhere with you, after the trick you pulled in china." She was watching him warily, and Sam knew that she was wondering just how far he would go.

Sam had never been a game-playing kind of man, but he realized he had developed a sudden fondness for playing games with this particular woman.

He took a deep breath and pretended to think about what she'd said. "Well, honey, if that's how you feel, there's only one thing I can do," he said after careful consideration.

Sam's arm whipped out to snare her, but Ginger had anticipated that move, and she leaped out of the way with a little squeal. The next thing he knew, she was darting into one of the book aisles. With a big grin, he followed her. She stayed carefully ahead of him, and he couldn't catch her without being obvious enough to make the clerks' heads turn again. He chuckled to himself. He definitely liked chasing his little rented Betty Crocker.

Sam took a different aisle, but Ginger noticed, and kept a shelf of books between them at all times. He began to slow down and look over some of the titles instead. He was in the mystery section, which suited him just fine. He'd been planning to stock up on some reading for the long winter ahead. But the image that came to mind was that of Ginger lying beside him in front of the fire while they both read. Maybe her head would be on his shoulder. He tried to wipe the grin from his face as he saw a cute little redhead ambling down the mystery aisle from the other end.

"I just love mysteries," the redhead said as she came to a stop and regarded him with a flirtatious smile. Her eyes ran down Sam's impressive height. Still smiling at him, she took a book from the shelf.

"So do I," he said, noting out of the corner of his

eye that Ginger was frowning at them from the next aisle.

"I usually read Sue Grafton," the redhead said, sidling closer and smiling at him.

"Good choice," he said. He mentioned a recent title, and the redhead agreed enthusiastically that it was a good read. Another sideways glance at Ginger almost made him smile. Her mouth was puckered, her brow furrowed, and she was keeping one eye on him while she paged through a book. He was curious to see what she would do about this.

He didn't have to wait long.

The redhead made another comment about Sue Grafton, and Ginger raised her head with determination.

"Look, darling," she cooed over the top of the shelf. "Isn't this the book the doctor told you to read before the honeymoon?"

She held up the book with a bright, innocent smile, and the redhead gasped audibly.

Sam tried not to laugh when he saw the title: *Living with Impotence.*

The redhead didn't even have a parting word for him. She was gone before he looked around again.

Ginger blew imaginary smoke from her finger. "Don't mess with me, cowboy," she warned him tartly.

Sam grinned. "Think you're pretty clever, don't you?" he asked.

"As a matter of fact, yes." She tossed her hair and continued her browsing.

A moment later, he held up another mystery. "Ever read this?" he asked.

Ginger peered over the shelf and smiled. "I *love* her."

A minute later, she was on his side of the shelf and they were trading reading recommendations. That image of her reading with him in front of the fire came to mind again, but he pushed it aside. He told himself that he wasn't going to get involved.

But in the meantime, he had to admit he really got a kick out of teasing her.

When Enid returned with Emily, she insisted on dragging them through the glasswares, picking out a set of wineglasses for Sam and Ginger. Sam noted with amusement that Ginger opened her mouth to protest, then closed it again after a quick glance at Sam. She didn't even protest when Enid decided that Emily needed a fancy glass piggy bank. In fact, the only hint of fireworks came when they passed the lingerie department on their way out.

Sam was carrying the large box of china, and Enid led the way, swinging her purse to clear a path in front of them, like a soldier with a bayonet.

She came to an abrupt halt in front of a lacy display of teddies and turned to Ginger. Ginger tried to focus on the men's underwear across the aisle and not the wispy fabric draped in front of her.

"Have you picked out anything for your trousseau?" Enid asked.

Ginger was too embarrassed to formulate a lie on the spot.

"I have a few things," she murmured. "I don't really need anything more."

"Nonsense," Enid insisted. "A girl can never have too much in the way of fancy underwear and nightgowns. Besides, even my backwoods son can appreciate lace and silk, can't you, dear?"

"I'm looking forward to seeing each and every scrap of lace," Sam assured her seriously.

Ginger shot him a warning frown as the heat began to climb her face yet again.

"What about this?" Enid asked, holding up a silvery-blue teddy that was little more than a scrap of lace held up by two straps. The tiniest of bows nestled between two see-through cups.

"Oh, my," Ginger whispered in dismay.

"Maybe you should go try it on," Sam suggested innocently, the devilment in his eyes obvious. "Just to make sure it fits."

Ginger spared him a sharp look. She thought this was a little out of character for him, given his criticism of her for not looking more like a homemaker. She decided he was determined to give her the business again.

Sam smiled to himself. He fully expected Ginger to wad up the teddy and throw it at him. That certainly would have been Denise's reaction.

But Betty Crocker surprised him once again. Taking a deep breath, she said, "I think this teddy will do nicely. And while we're at it, let's take this too." She took two steps and pulled a pair of skimpy men's bikini briefs in a leopard print from a nearby hook. Dangling them from one finger in front of Sam's face, she said, "I can't wait to see you in this, darling."

Sam swallowed his chuckle and hid behind the box. She was full of surprises.

9

Ginger was so worn out by the trip to St. Louis that she quickly fell into a deep sleep at home that night. Emily had nodded off in the car, and Ginger had half carried her inside.

When she woke abruptly, Ginger rolled over, looked at the clock and groaned. Three in the morning. She was still tired, but she knew that sleep was beyond her now.

It was the dream that had done it. Another dream about Sam. It had been a stupid dream, really, a fantasy brought about by exhaustion and too much sugar. But explaining it didn't make it go away.

She dragged the pillow over her head and tried to block out the remembered feel of his hands on her. But it didn't fade. Neither would the heat in her body, the heat her overactive libido had generated from the fantasy.

They had been walking in a meadow filled with wildflowers. It had been the kind of setting that on television would be a butter commercial.

Sam's fingers had been linked with hers. They had stopped, and Sam had tugged her down into the thick grass with him. His fingers had tangled in her hair and held her head still as his mouth plundered hers. She had groaned with the intensity of her sudden arousal. She had arched her back, pressing her breasts into his chest, and immediately his hands and mouth had been everywhere on her body. Miraculously, her clothes had melted away, and she'd lain naked beneath him.

But, just as Sam's wonderful hands aroused her to a fever pitch, Enid's trilling voice had washed over them. "Sam! Ginger! Come to dinner! I made tofu." And Ginger had lain there completely naked as Enid began singing at the top of her lungs. *"Yes, we have no tofu."*

She was going crazy. That was the only explanation. She never used to have such bizarre dreams. She used to be a contented homemaker and mother, whose idea of an exciting evening was knitting an afghan while she watched a television sitcom with her husband.

And then, when she was widowed, the exciting evenings had become a pasta salad and a good book.

Now, she was the pretend fiancée of a big, teasing cowboy who inspired ridiculous erotic dreams. Sighing, she got out of bed and opened the shopping bag that still lay on her dresser. Holding up the teddy in the dim light from the hall, she sighed again. She hadn't even been able to put it in the drawer with her other lingerie, almost as if she feared her plain white underwear would turn pink with embarrassment.

Oh, she was one unhinged woman, all right. And it was all Sam Weller's fault.

"You know," Emily said on the ride to Sam's ranch the next morning, Sunday. "Sam's mom buys neat stuff for girls. Like my piggy bank. How come she bought Sam all the wrong stuff when he was a little boy?"

The question surprised Ginger. She hadn't thought

that Emily would remember the clarinet and the bicycle from the barn. She realized that Emily deserved a serious answer.

"I don't think she knew much about boys, honey. She didn't know what they liked."

Emily thought about that, then shook her head. "I think she wanted Sam to be like her instead of his father."

Ginger looked at her daughter in surprise. Now where had that adult observation come from?

"How do you figure that?" Ginger asked carefully.

Emily sighed. "When I asked her what it was like when she was a little girl, she said she lived in the city. She said she liked music and clothes and movies. But her mom always got her stuff like a tennis racquet for her birthday. She said she didn't have anybody who liked the same things she did." Emily took a deep breath to continue her speech. "I think maybe she got a clarinet for Sam because no one got her what she really wanted when she was a little girl, and she wanted someone else to like the stuff she did."

"I think you're right," Ginger said softly, reaching over to caress Emily's cheek with the back of her fingers. "You're something, you know that?"

Emily giggled. "Huh-uh. Sam says *you're* the one who's something."

Ginger tried not to smile, but she wasn't entirely successful. Somewhere along the way, she had begun to enjoy the verbal sparring with Sam.

Enid had just come downstairs when Ginger and Emily arrived, and Ginger set about fixing breakfast, tying her white apron around her waist. Sam came in from the back of the house and gave her a long, lingering look before setting his baseball cap on the counter. It gave Ginger a lift to see him wearing it, because she knew he was doing it for her.

"Let me help," he murmured, getting out the knives, forks and napkins.

Sam moved wordlessly to the skillet to take over turning the bacon while Ginger poured scrambled eggs into another skillet. She brushed close to him, and he caught a tantalizing whiff of her violet-scented soap. At that moment, he could have cheerfully carried her upstairs to his bed, were it not for Enid and Emily.

It was driving him crazy to be so close to her all the time and not do more than give her a teasing kiss now and then. Last night, he had dreamed of that damn teddy his mother bought for Ginger, and he had awoken in a painful state.

It had been more than the prospect of more hot cottage cheese for breakfast that prompted his offer of help in the kitchen. He liked being near her. Actually, he *needed* to be near her. When he wasn't thinking about wrapping his hands around her neck because of the way she was teasing him, he was thinking about wrapping his mouth around other parts of her body and sating himself on her charms.

As if she could read the erotic turn his thoughts had taken, Ginger glanced at him from under her lashes and flushed.

Ginger put the breakfast on the table, and Sam's eyes followed her grimly. He sat down, but couldn't manage more than a couple of bites. He toyed with his fork, glowering at nothing, while he tried to drive away the images of Ginger's hair spilled around her head on his pillow. His face was unexpressive when he glanced at Ginger.

He was in that mood again, Ginger thought, mentally bracing herself. He was as cranky as he'd been at the beginning of the trip to St. Louis yesterday. She wasn't sure whether it was something she'd done or something she hadn't done, but she could see definite annoyance in his eyes. The man was a mystery to her. Maybe it was the apron that was irritating him. Then again, maybe it was the way the sun had risen this morning.

Ginger noticed that he wasn't eating, and, truth to tell, her appetite wasn't up to snuff this morning, either. It was that stupid dream. Why couldn't she dream simple, uncomplicated dreams about eating her weight in chocolate or winning the lottery, instead of that mixed-up mishmash of Sam and Enid?

Sam pushed back his chair ten minutes after they all began to eat.

"The horses need some exercise, Mother," he said shortly. "Ginger and I are going to go do it."

She shot him a look of alarm, but he stopped her with his steady gaze. Obviously, it was important that she go riding with him.

"But, dear," Enid said, "I think it's too dangerous to take Ginger."

Amen to that, Ginger agreed to herself.

"She knows how to ride a horse," Sam told her, giving Ginger another look that dared her to contradict him.

"Is that right, dear?" Enid asked Ginger.

Ginger nodded. "Years of riding lessons," she mumbled. "Reins, saddles, currycombs..." She smiled wanly. She had told so many lies since she met Sam that she was going to have to join a convent to atone.

Sam had taken her hand and begun to pull her toward the door when he noticed Emily's stricken face.

"What is it, Em?" he asked, frowning.

It was clear from her trembling lip that she was upset.

"But I *love* to ride horses," she said in a pleading voice. "Can't I go with you?"

Sam softened immediately. "Of course you can. Come on."

"Well," Enid said with a sigh, "I'll be standing by the phone if you need a doctor."

Ginger's heart was thumping wildly as Sam led them toward the pasture. Emily danced alongside, excited.

Sam looked every inch the cowboy this morning. His jeans were worn but still formfitting, and his blue chambray shirt strained over his muscular shoulders. The familiar black hat was back, pulled low over his eyes.

Two horses nickered at Sam's approach and sidled up to the fence. He disappeared momentarily into the barn and emerged with two halters. He talked to Emily as he haltered the horses and led them to the barn, but he seemed to be ignoring Ginger on purpose. She was more than rattled by the prospect of getting up on one of those four-legged skyscrapers, and he wasn't helping any.

When the horses were saddled and bridled, Ginger hung back, even when Sam beckoned to her with one finger.

"Not nervous, are you?" he asked, with the first hint of amusement. "Here, just put your foot in the stirrup, and I'll boost you on up. By the way, her name's Firecracker."

Ginger came to a full stop with her foot in the air. *"Firecracker?"* She turned to look at him with such a panicked look that he laughed.

"Because she was born on the Fourth of July. Nothing to do with her temperament."

"You wouldn't have a guarantee to that effect, would you?"

"Sorry." He was still grinning.

"Then how about some super glue?"

His eyebrows went up quizzically.

"That's the only thing that will keep my seat on that saddle," she lamented.

"But what about those years of riding lessons?" he teased her.

"Oh, they were all for foxhunting or something," she said with a wave of her hand. "Nothing like this."

"I see." He regarded her gravely. "What kind of an example are you setting for little Miss Emily here?" he asked gently. "Do you want her to grow up frightened of new experiences?"

As far as Ginger could see, Emily was anything but frightened by the prospect of riding a horse. Ginger, on the other hand, had always been a little timid about large animals, especially ones that had a reputation for racing away, dragging their hapless riders by one foot.

But Firecracker was regarding her dolefully from big brown eyes, and Ginger couldn't find it in herself to be too afraid. She planted her foot in the stirrup and let Sam boost her up. He adjusted her feet, then showed her how to hold the reins.

"Just touch her with the rein like this," he said, demonstrating, "and she'll turn. She's as gentle as they come, and well trained. Nudge her with your heels to get her going."

"Fine," she said shortly, gripping the reins in her fists, her back ramrod-straight.

"And, Ginger?" he said, swinging up into the saddle

of the other horse, then boosting Emily to sit in front of him. He waited until she took her eyes off the reins to look at him, and then he grinned. "Don't let her get too close to the stream."

Ginger's eyes were round. "Why? Will she jump it?"

Sam's laugh was deep in his chest. "No, honey. It's just that she likes to eat watercress."

Sam took the lead, and they rode leisurely and quietly for a while, Sam leaning down to open and close the gate when they moved into the pasture. His horse grew restless when they slowed, and he began to prance, but Sam kept him under control. Ginger actually managed to relax, so much so that at one point she got so caught up in watching a hawk soar in the sky that she let one foot slide out of the stirrup. Firecracker stopped immediately and looked back at her, like a patient teacher waiting for a charge to pay attention.

As they crossed the stream, Sam was pointing out things to Emily, and she was squealing delightedly at everything around them. Ginger realized that they were in the pasture where they had picnicked, and when they came over a low rise, she saw the lake ahead. They had approached it from a different angle this time, and the sunlight danced on it like brilliant sequins.

"Is that where you fish, Sam?" Emily asked, pointing toward the run-down dock jutting into the lake and toppling under the water at the end.

"A long time ago, Em," Sam said quietly.

"Can I go see it?"

"All right," he said, helping her down. "But stay on the shore. The dock's not very sturdy."

Sam dismounted, then reached up to help Ginger.

"I'm not sure I should get down," she said hesitantly. "I may not make it back up again."

Sam arched a brow at her and reached up to lift her off. She was pressed against his chest a long moment before he let her slide down the length of his hard body. She couldn't seem to catch her breath while he watched her.

"I'm going to demand that you pay me a bonus, you know," she said, with more bravado than she felt.

"For riding a horse?" He regarded her with amusement.

"No, for the therapy I'm going to need. You're driving me insane. I have never known a man as moody as you."

"Moody? I'm not moody." His frown was returning.

"Oh, you are definitely moody," she informed him. "Talk about Jekyll and Hyde. One minute you're as nice as Roy Rogers, and the next you turn into Jesse James on a two-day funk."

"*I* do this?" he said in disbelief, thumbing his hat back on his head.

"I don't know—maybe it's a chemical imbalance, or you're just not a morning person. You were definitely crabby when we left for St. Louis yesterday, and you were no picnic this morning, either. I asked Firecracker what your problem was, but she didn't have any answers." She had thrown that last comment in to lighten the mood, because he was getting a very dark look in his eyes.

"*This* is what my problem is," he said quietly, and the next thing she knew, she was pulled tightly to his chest again, only this time his mouth was descending toward hers. She gave a soft gasp just before his lips tasted hers. There was something different about the way he kissed her this time. There was a hunger that hadn't been there before. And she was unable to put up any kind of resistance—not that she wanted to.

Sam's horse screened them from Emily's view, and Sam's hands ran over her possessively. When his finger and thumb stroked her nipple through her blouse, she shivered with heat.

"*I'm* the one who's going insane," Sam growled against her throat, his mouth marauding there and making a soft moan issue from her throat. "And if my mother doesn't give us some privacy, I'm going to plead insanity at the murder trial after I kill her."

Ginger's laugh turned into a groan as his hands found her breasts again. "Emily," she managed to say.

Sam looked around the horse, then said, "She's fine. She's picking up rocks."

Ginger stood still, half expecting him to kiss her again, and too hungry for his touch to pretend she didn't want it. She was able to fabricate lies for his mother out of thin air, but she was finding it increasingly difficult to lie to this man.

When he didn't say anything, only continued to look at her, she grew nervous.

"Did you build the dock yourself?" she asked, reaching for anything to dispel the tension between them.

Sam nodded. "Denise thought it would be great to have parties here by the lake." He made no attempt to hide the disgust in his voice. "She said she wanted a swimming pool by the house, but when I didn't come through with that she decided to make the lake the setting for her entertaining."

Ginger sighed. "It's too intimate a place for big parties.'' She gazed out at the lake, feeling a languor wash over her. ''You know what it needs?''

''Yeah. A portable bar. That was high on Denise's list.''

Ginger laughed and shook her head. ''No, it needs a gazebo. Right there at the end of the dock. Can't you imagine sitting in a gazebo on a summer night, with the stars swimming above and the moon reflected on the water? My grandmother had a gazebo in her yard when I was a little girl. I loved it. I always wanted one of my own—one with a stained-glass window in it.''

''I'm sure the mosquitoes would enjoy it too,'' he said dryly.

Ginger swatted his arm. ''You have no romance in your soul,'' she told him with a mock sigh.

Sam gave her a smoldering look that contained a dare. ''Tell me that when we're alone, honey.''

Even though she could see his eyes, she still wasn't sure whether he was teasing her or not. But she decided to be bold.

''Yeah?'' she said softly. ''You get us alone, cowboy, and I'll be glad to repeat it.'' She nearly regretted it the moment the words left her lips. Did he guess how much she longed to have him make love to her?

Sam's smile was slow and warm. ''We'll see,'' he said enigmatically.

As soon as he had the horses unsaddled, brushed and turned out to pasture again, Sam snatched up the cell phone he kept in the barn and dialed Jeannie's number.

''What are you doing?'' he asked as soon as she picked up the phone.

''Making jelly and baby-sitting a friend's poodle while she goes apartment hunting,'' she said. ''Why?''

"I think you ought to call Mother and invite her and Emily to lunch. After all, you should get to spend as much quality time with her as I am."

"Getting on your nerves, is she?" Jeannie asked in amusement. "This is going to cost you, you know."

"It already has," he retorted. "And be sure to invite Emily too."

"Wait a minute," Jeannie said in amusement. "You have an ulterior motive in this little invitation, don't you, big brother? Just what do you have planned for Ginger?"

"None of your business," he said bluntly.

"All right," Jeannie said, laughing. "I'll bail you out. Just remember that you owe me a favor."

A few minutes after he hung up, the phone rang again, and he let them pick it up in the house.

"Jeannie is going to take Emily and me to lunch!" Enid announced brightly when he walked into the kitchen fifteen minutes later. "I tried to get Ginger to come along, but she said there are some things around here she needs to do."

Sam's eyes slid to Ginger, but she wouldn't look at him, and he detected a pinkness high on her cheekbones.

"Jeannie's got a dog!" Emily announced excitedly. "She said I can pet it."

"Have fun, then," Ginger said, and she managed to smile as Jeannie's car pulled into the driveway.

Her tension was an odd mixture of longing and anxiety. She wanted Sam with a raw need that was almost painful, but she was so afraid he might see her love for him on her face. She knew it would be a disaster if he ever found out that she had fallen in love with him. No doubt he would terminate their pretend engagement as soon as possible, maybe even before his mother left.

As soon as Enid and Emily were gone, Sam went upstairs without a word to her, and she felt a stab of disappointment. Hormone overload, she told herself. Well, she would just have to get over it. Apparently, Sam Weller didn't plan to do anything more erotic than tease her with his kisses.

Deciding that work would be more constructive than sitting around like a lovesick teen, Ginger got out the step stool and climbed it to finish some quick hand-stitching on the hem she had only pinned before. She didn't hear Sam come back downstairs, and she went on with her work, oblivious to him standing behind her, his eyes taking in every detail of her appearance. Her black jeans had a small smudge of dirt on the seat from the horseback ride, and her turquoise pullover sweater tightened over her breasts. The light from the window made her hair shimmer with coppery highlights. There was a fresh outdoors scent about her that was as intoxicating as any perfume.

Sam reached out and traced his finger down her spine. Ginger jumped and spun around on the stool, nearly toppling off. In an instant, his hands were at her waist to steady her. She stared down at him, the needle and thread still in her hand.

They stared at each other a long moment, and Ginger could hear the mantel clock in the living room ticking steadily. It was far slower than her heartbeat.

"Say it," he said gruffly, and though she knew he was teasing her, there was no humor in his eyes.

Ginger swallowed and pretended not to understand. She was suddenly nervous all over again, and she was trying to buy time.

"Say what?"

Sam smiled slowly. "You, Ginger Marsh, are a coward."

"I am not." Still, she couldn't quite meet his eyes.

"Then say it," he drawled. "I dare you."

"Is that a single dare or a double dare?" she parried.

Sam's smile widened. "It's the biggest dare you've ever had in your life, honey. Now, are you going to say it, or are you going to wimp out on me?"

She just stood there and stared back at him, her heart hammering in her throat.

Sam gave a muffled laugh. "Thought so," he said. "You're definitely a chicken."

He turned to leave, and when he had taken two steps, Ginger took a deep breath and said what he was waiting to hear. "Sam Weller, you don't have a romantic bone in your body."

He stopped in his tracks and turned to face her, his eyes dancing with devilment. "Oh, I've got one or two I'd like to show you, sweetheart." Then he scooped her up in his arms, making her squeal. She nearly poked herself in the hand with the needle. "You won't be needing that," he told her, taking it from her and dropping it on the table on his way to the stairs.

"Oh, I don't know," she said tartly, deciding he needed some teasing after all the aggravation he'd just given her. "I might get bored."

Sam laughed again. "Want to bet?"

No, she didn't, because she was pretty sure this was one bet she would lose. Bored was the last thing she expected to be.

Sam set her down on the first step and looked at her hungrily, his hands smoothing over her hips. Ginger stared into his darkening eyes and felt her blood heat even more. She traced his lips with her finger.

"What's wrong?" she whispered. "Not strong enough to make it all the way upstairs?"

He grinned and shook his head. "Haven't been eating my oysters, sweetheart."

She laughed then—a laugh that turned into a shriek as he ducked down and hoisted her over his shoulder. She was still laughing as he carried her into his bedroom and laid her on the bed.

He was looming over her, and his sheer size alone was intimidating. But this was Sam, and Ginger felt nothing but an increasing desire.

Sam's finger caught her sweater at the bottom and began to tug it upward. But Ginger had something else in mind.

"Wait," she said in a husky voice. "Take your clothes off first." When he looked at her in surprise, she whispered, "I dare you."

Sam's slow smile spread over his face. "I believe I'll take that dare," he drawled, and reached for his own shirt, tugging it out of his waistband and quickly undoing the buttons.

Ginger's eyes widened as he pulled the shirt off impatiently and tossed it aside. She had seen his chest before, but never when he was about to make love to her. His sheer animal power was mesmerizing.

"Enjoying yourself?" he murmured as he kicked off his shoes and unzipped his jeans.

She could only nod. *Oh, yes. Oh, my.*

"I have to warn you," he said carefully as he began to take off the jeans. To Ginger's surprise, he actually looked worried. "I'm not as young as I used to be."

"I know—you're older than dirt," she told him tartly. "But I'm no kid, either."

He smiled, then stood naked before her and let her look all she wanted.

Sam sat down on the edge of the bed and reached for her sweater again. She lay still as he pulled it over her head, but when his hands drifted to her breasts, her breath caught in her throat. His eyes holding hers, Sam stroked her nipples to pebble-hardness before slipping her bra straps from her shoulders.

When she was naked to the waist, he lowered his mouth to her nipple and laved it with his tongue. Ginger groaned and clutched his shoulders. She was so lost in his touch that she didn't even notice that he had unzipped her jeans until he whispered for her to lift her hips. The jeans landed on the floor, with her panties soon following.

She lay naked beneath him, staring up at his hard, muscled body and marveling at how gentle he was with her. He stroked her everywhere with his hands and with his mouth, until she was squirming beneath him, her breath escaping in small gasps.

She slid her hands down his chest and to his waist, then lower, feeling a spurt of pleasure when he groaned as she touched him. She stroked him the way he had stroked her, and Sam kissed her urgently.

"Slow down, honey," he murmured, "or this will be over in record time."

"I don't want to go slow," she whispered, realizing that it was true. "You're driving me crazy."

"Me too," he said, stroking her cheek with his finger. "But let's see if I can't make you even crazier." With a wicked smile, he lowered his hand, his fingers working magic where she was most vulnerable.

"Oh!" she gasped, squirming. "Oh, Sam!"

When she thought she couldn't take another wonderful, sweet, aching second of this onslaught, he sat up and opened the drawer of the nightstand.

"I was afraid I didn't have any of these around," he murmured, drawing out the foil packet. "It's been years."

Ginger didn't even realize what Sam had until he began to unwrap it, and then she flushed.

"I hope they're not moldy," she said, only half joking.

Sam laughed. "Honey, they're not the only thing in danger of being a little the worse for disuse."

Ginger flushed again. "You look fine to me," she managed to say, her breath hissing out, as Sam positioned himself between her legs and gently probed.

"You keep that in mind, sweetheart," he told her, brushing back her hair as he kissed her. "I'm trying to go slow for you, but I'm not made of steel. I may not be too good at this anymore. And I'm not as—"

"Right. You're ancient. Now stop stalling, cowboy."

He took infinite pains to pleasure her, something that made her feel special and a little embarrassed. But the sheer sensuality of what he was doing to her soon drove away the embarrassment.

Sam moved slowly inside her, and she loved the feeling. Then his hand slid between them to stroke her on the outside even as he stroked her on the inside, and she nearly cried with the sudden waves of pleasure building within her.

"Sam," she murmured, clutching at him and arching.

"That's it, honey," he whispered, his own breathing raspy. "Let yourself go."

And she did just as he bid her. The feelings spiraled out of control, and she cried out. Sam was groaning the next minute, and then he gently rolled to her side, pulling her into his arms.

"No doubt about it," she said softly when she caught her breath. "I think you might just be a champion, blue-ribbon lovemaking cowboy."

10

When Jeannie called Sam that afternoon to report that she was about to bring Enid and Emily back, Sam tried to sound as casual as he could.

"Fine," he said. "Did they have a good time?"

Jeannie cleared her throat. "Yes, I think they did."

Sam could sense that there was something Jeannie wasn't telling him, and he frowned. "And?"

Jeannie coughed slightly. "Nothing. We'll be there shortly."

But when the car pulled into the drive and Enid and Emily got out, Jeannie left so quickly that a haze of dust obscured her car from view. Now Sam was sure she was up to something. He didn't have to wait long to find out what it was.

Emily came racing into the house with a white bundle of squirming fluff.

"Look, Sam!" she cried. "Look what Jeannie's giving you!"

Sam glanced at his mother before he looked back at the bundle, but Enid was pointedly studying everything in the house except him.

"What is that?" Sam asked calmly.

Emily giggled. "It's a poodle, Sam."

"And why is that...poodle here?" He was making

an effort to keep his temper under control, since he was dealing with Emily at the moment. But if he got his hands on his sister...

Enid finally stepped forward. "Jeannie's friend found an apartment, but they won't take dogs, so I thought that Noelle could keep Ratso company."

"You thought," Sam said ominously.

Enid looked discomfited. "Well, it was really Jeannie's idea, but it seemed like the logical thing to do. Sam, that dog of yours needs another interest."

"Mother, it's not like I can enroll him in night classes or something. He's a dog. He's *supposed* to lie around."

Enid raised a skeptical brow. "I don't think it's healthy for any animal to lie around that much. I'm beginning to wonder if he doesn't have thyroid trouble. I ought to look that up in my herb book."

"You do that," he said grimly. Then he turned to say something to Emily, but she had already gone to the front door, where Ratso was lying. He hadn't even opened his eyes when Enid and Emily came in and stepped over him. He might have been mistaken for dead, if not for the soft snoring sounds he was making.

Emily knelt beside him and lowered the poodle to the floor. "Look what we brought you, Ratso," she crooned. "A brand-new friend. Won't you have fun?"

Ratso opened one eye and regarded the poodle skeptically. For her part, the poodle sniffed the air delicately, then gave a genteel snuff and a shake of her head. She stretched in front of Ratso, then pulled up one corner of the rug and began to chew it.

Ratso and Sam groaned at the same time.

* * *

As Ginger drove to Sam's ranch on Monday afternoon, Emily sat pensively by her side, her small brows knit in a frown.

"What's the matter, darling?" Ginger asked. "Tough day at school?"

Emily shook her head. "No, we had the bookmobile there today. And I got a book out." She dug in her book bag and held a book up for Ginger, who took her eyes off the road just long enough to catch the title.

Dog Training for Beginners.

"Since Sam put me in charge of Noelle, I figured I needed some help," Emily explained.

"Sweetie, I think we're all in need of help with that poodle around," Ginger said, laughing.

"Want me to read it to you?" Emily asked.

"Sure. Go ahead." She listened indulgently as Emily carefully read the instructions in the book. One point became immediately clear. Dogs responded to praise.

Be lavish in your praise when your dog did what you want, the book recommended, and quick to show that you didn't like unacceptable behavior. The best method for dealing with one of your dog's bad habits was to say no loudly and remove the dog from the scene of the crime. Let your dog know that you loved him, but there were things you will not tolerate.

As they pulled into the ranch drive, Ginger idly wondered whether the same training technique would work on men.

She had been worrying all night about what to do where Sam was concerned. If she had been in love with him before they made love, she was hopelessly drowning in it now. He had been tender and funny and captivating, all at the same time. And she knew that if he sensed how much she loved him, she would experience zero gravity from the speed with which he would get her out of his life.

As soon as Sam came in from the pasture, Ginger could see that he was in one of his sulks. He barely glanced at her, and when he did, his dark brows drew together. She knew that it was a reflexive action from their intimacy. She had learned that much about Sam. For every breach made in his wall, he threw up two new bricks. She didn't know whether it was possible to train a man into emotional intimacy, but she was darn well going to give it her best shot.

Enid looked up as Sam entered the kitchen and sighed. Apparently, she had given up trying to deal with his moods. She went back to snapping green beans with a shake of her head.

Sam flung his hat on the counter and pulled out a chair. Ginger took a deep breath, then turned away from the stove with a spatula in her hand.

"Sam," she said with a tinge of iron in her voice, "please put your hat on the rack and wipe that frown off your face. Dinner's almost ready."

He stared at her in shock, but after a moment frozen in his chair, he got up and hung up the hat. When he turned back to her, he was clearly taken aback.

"Is this better?" he asked. He wasn't smiling, but Ginger could see the amusement in his eyes.

"Much," she told him. When she glanced at Enid, Ginger saw that her mouth was gaping open.

Lesson one, Ginger thought in satisfaction.

In the living room, Emily said loudly, "Good girl, Noelle. Good dog." Ginger flushed and went back to her skillet.

Sam was in a much better mood throughout dinner,

and Ginger began to think that he just needed someone to stand up to him. After all, he had been living alone for several years, and he was used to having everything done his own way.

He offered to take everyone out for ice cream after dinner, and Ginger made a point of smiling at him and telling him how nice it was of him to offer.

He gave her a suspicious look on the way to the truck, as if he were trying to figure out what she was up to, but he helped her inside with good humor and drove them all to town.

They passed the bridal store as they walked to the ice cream shop, and Ginger shot a sideways glance at the champagne-colored two-piece dress in the window. It was just the style she liked, a silky, clinging top with a lacy high collar and fitted sleeves. The skirt was straight, but softly pleated, and hung to the ankles. Running the length of the blouse and continuing down the skirt was a row of tiny pearl buttons. Soft and feminine but stylish, it would be perfect with flowers in the hair or a hat.

"Isn't that beautiful?" Enid asked, pausing to admire the dress. She held one hand to her heart, as if the mere sight made it flutter.

"Very nice," Ginger agreed.

They were all moving on when the shop door opened and Mavis Andrews popped her head out to call to them.

"I heard about your engagement, Ginger," she said with a big grin. "I put this dress in the window specifically for you."

"It's lovely," Ginger told her.

"Oh, try it on, dear," Enid urged Ginger. "I'd love to see how it looks on you."

Ginger looked at Sam helplessly, but he shrugged, and she capitulated. She avoided the mirror while she was slipping the skirt over her head in the dressing room, and she kept her eyes tightly shut as she put on the top.

She stood there a long moment, staring down at the row of tiny buttons, then sighed. She had to look in a mirror sometime.

And when she did, she felt something grow quiet inside her. Staring back at her was a young woman with pinkened cheeks and reddish-blond hair that fell around her shoulders like sunshine and fire. The dress was everything she had imagined. It skimmed her hips and promised curves beneath. It glided over her shoulders and breasts and gently cupped the feminine contours. It was a dress for a bride, but a bride whose innocence was of the heart.

"Hurry up, dear!" Enid called. "I can't wait to see!"

Taking a deep breath, Ginger stepped out of the dressing room where Mavis, Enid, Emily and Sam stood waiting. Sam's hands were in his pockets, and he looked anything but comfortable. But when he saw her, his mouth worked, then closed abruptly. There was something in his eyes that might have been admiration, but he looked away when he caught her watching him.

"Oh, it's perfect!" Enid said, enraptured. "You look so beautiful. Doesn't she look beautiful, Sam? Oh, I forgot—you're not supposed to see her in it. Turn your back, Sam."

Sam muttered something, but Enid was too entranced with the dress to notice his lack of enthusiasm. "That's the dress for you, Ginger. I can't even imagine another one looking half this good. You do like it, don't you?''

Ginger smiled. ''Of course I do. I've never seen such a gorgeous wedding dress. It's perfect. It's just that…'' She glanced at Sam helplessly, but he was studying a selection of lace handkerchiefs, his back to her. He had picked a fine time to listen to his mother. Apparently, she would get no help from him. Now where were her glib lies when she needed them? ''A wedding dress is such a big commitment,'' she said carefully.

''My dear,'' Enid said with a twinkle in her eye as she put her hand on Ginger's arm, ''a *marriage* is a big commitment. The dress is something that will become a treasured memory. Think of it that way.''

Ginger smiled. ''You're right.''

''Then this is the dress?'' Enid asked with the excitement of a child.

''I love it, Mom,'' Emily piped up, and Ginger gave her hand a squeeze.

Ginger turned to Mavis, feeling trapped. ''How about if I put a deposit on the dress to hold it?'' she asked carefully. *And cancel it a week from now?*

Mavis squealed. ''Oh, I just knew you'd like it. It looks like it was made for you.''

Ginger went back to the dressing room, and as she opened the door and looked in the mirror, she saw Sam's reflection at the other end of the shop. He had turned from the handkerchiefs and was watching her with a frown.

She gave him a small shrug in the mirror, then closed the door. There had been speculation in his eyes, and more than a little wariness. And, sure enough, when she came out in her street clothes, Sam was in one of his moods.

Ginger was irritated herself by now. He could have helped her a little more with his mother and the wedding dress. Simply bowing to his mother's reminder of tradition and turning his back on the whole thing wasn't gallant, and it wasn't in character for Sam. Ginger found her own temper on edge.

"You all go ahead and get ice cream," Sam said when they stepped outside into the cooling air. "I think I'll take a walk by the river."

But Ginger was having none of that.

"It was your idea," she reminded him, with a gentleness that belied the steel behind the words. "Don't disappoint us now."

He looked at her for a long moment, then slowly followed them into the shop. But he covertly kept his eyes on Ginger. That woman had no idea what she was doing to him. She was turning him inside out, and making love to her had only increased his frustration. Damn! He'd told her how things were with him. But he could still see the dreams in her eyes.

It might kill him, but he was going to walk away from Ginger Marsh and her cute little daughter when his mother went back home. And the sooner Ginger realized that was how it was going to be, the better.

"I'll take the chocolate," he said without spirit after everyone else had been served.

Ginger looked up at him with a challenging tilt to her chin. "Make it a double," she said in a low voice. "You need it."

"You don't know anything about what I need right now, honey," he murmured quietly.

"I think I do," she insisted, with that streak of stubbornness he was beginning to recognize.

"Yeah, we'll see." He turned his back on her, only

this time it was from irritation and not respect for a tradition. Ginger's temper was rising quickly.

She kept herself in check until they got back to the ranch, but as soon as Enid was upstairs reading and Emily was on the porch reading a story to a fidgety Noelle and a sleeping Ratso, Ginger went out the back door toward the barn. She had watched Sam head that way not ten minutes ago, and she was determined to stand up to him about his insufferable attitude.

Ginger paused in the doorway, frowning into the light. She heard the crunching of hay and the swishing of a tail against a wooden stall, but she didn't see Sam.

"What are you doing out here?" he demanded from behind her, and she jumped.

When she turned around, she saw him silhouetted in the open doorway, his cowboy hat pulled down low over his eyes. He was carrying a bucket of some kind of feed, and he strode past her with it, disappearing into a stall on the left.

Ginger edged closer. Peering inside, she saw Sam pouring the feed into a trough. Firecracker stood patiently, waiting for him to finish. He patted the horse on the shoulder as he stepped around her, and she nickered in response.

Sam didn't look at Ginger until he had closed the stall door. "Well?" he said gruffly, his hands on his hips.

Ginger took a deep breath. "I want to know why you're so angry tonight," she said quickly, before she could lose her nerve.

"And what makes you think I'm angry?" he asked. There was no change in his tone, but his jaw had tightened, she noticed.

"Because I've seen you do this every time something gets through your carefully constructed wall, every time I get close to you.''

"Is that what you think you are?" he demanded. "Close to me?"

"I might be, if you'd let me," she snapped back. "But ever since we went to bed together, you've acted like I'm one huge inconvenience to you. And I don't like it.''

"Why should it bother you?"

"Because I…'' *Because I love you.* "Because I do care for you, and I don't like to see you like this.''

Sam didn't say anything for so long that Ginger was afraid that she'd pushed him too far, that he would never give her any kind of answer. Frustration made her resort to a challenge.

"What's the matter?" she said mockingly. "Don't you have the guts to be honest for once?"

Sam's jaw tightened even more. "You want honesty?" he snapped. "All right. I'll give you what you want, Ginger. But I'm warning you—you won't like it. You want to know why I've been giving you the cold shoulder tonight? Because of that damn wedding dress, that's why."

"What do you mean?" She hid her hands behind her back, so that he couldn't see them trembling.

"Did you really think I couldn't read the look in your eyes, Ginger? You're not very good at hiding your emotions. Your face was an open book after we made love. I told myself that it was just the physical closeness. But then I saw that look on your face again when you went to change out of that wedding dress. You're—''

"Stop it!" she said quickly. "I don't want to hear any more.''

"Sorry, honey," he said, with real sympathy in his voice. "But you wanted to know." He pushed the hat back, and for the first time she saw that there was a sadness in his eyes that she hadn't expected. "I don't want a wedding, Ginger. I don't want to see you coming down the aisle in that dress, not even with that sweet look in your eyes. And I don't want to bring you home to this ranch, no matter how much you might think you love me now. Because I know what will happen. Those are your dreams, not mine. I'm sorry all of this is going to hurt you, but that's the way it is. I never pretended otherwise."

She felt as if a knife were turning inside her. *He knew that she loved him.* She had never felt so sick or so humiliated in her life.

"I understand," she said stiffly, clenching her teeth to keep them from chattering. She abruptly spun on her heel and hurried out of the barn.

He didn't try to stop her, though he felt as if someone had punched him in the stomach.

11

Sam barely spoke to Ginger the next afternoon, when she showed up at the ranch after Emily got home from school. He tersely informed her that Jeannie had picked up Enid to have a late lunch with her in town. Ginger nodded, then brushed past him and went straight to the kitchen. He was paying her to be a maid, and that was what she would be, she told herself.

Now that he had guessed how she felt about him, Ginger decided she'd been embarrassed as much as possible. She could hear faint hammering sounds from somewhere in the vicinity of the pasture, but she resolutely tried to keep her mind off Sam Weller and his surliness.

She was cooking beef stew and getting out flour for biscuits when she heard Jeannie's car. Enid popped her head into the kitchen long enough to inhale the aroma before she went upstairs to take a nap.

Jeannie sighed when she came in and tossed her purse on a chair. "Mother didn't sleep at all last night," she said. "Noelle howled until morning. And Sam's in a foul mood, as well." She leaned on the counter and ran a hand through her hair. "Everything's screwed up."

That much was true, but Ginger suspected that Sam's

mood had more to do with their confrontation than with Noelle's vocalizations.

"I suppose Sam's yelled at you, too, this afternoon," Jeannie said apologetically. "He certainly couldn't wait for the car to stop before he gave me a piece of his mind about Noelle."

"Oh, he took care of yelling at me last night," Ginger said, sighing herself. When Jeannie gave her a curious look, Ginger said, "He thinks I have marriage on my mind."

"Oh." Jeannie chewed her lower lip. She looked so guilty that Ginger wondered if Noelle wasn't just the tip of Jeannie's troubles with Sam.

"Your mother had me try on a wedding dress last night," Ginger said. "It set Sam off like a fireworks display."

Jeannie drummed her fingers on the counter and frowned. "He's just not used to the idea," she said, almost to herself.

"What do you mean?" Now Ginger was frowning. Jeannie sounded as if she expected there really would be a wedding.

Jeannie looked at Ginger and seemed to collect herself.

"I just mean that it's such a change for him, having a woman around here." She glanced toward the back. "Hey, where's Emily?"

"You won't believe this," Ginger assured her as she led the way out the back door. "She's been training Noelle."

Jeannie whooped with laughter when she came outside and peered from behind Ginger. Emily had set up a miniature tea party on a blanket on the grass. A small table sat in the middle with a teacup and saucer on

three sides. Noelle sat on one side, her topknot decorated with a red silk rose attached to a stretchable band
that looped around the poodle's chin. She was looking
expectantly at the box of dog biscuits in the center of
the table.

Across from the poodle was Ratso, a tiny felt hat on
his head, secured in the same manner, and a small bow
tie at his neck. Though less intense than the poodle's,
Ratso's eyes were also on the treats.

Emily sat cross-legged on her side of the table, dabbing at her mouth with a napkin.

"May I offer you another cookie, Miss Noelle?" she
asked, holding out a dog biscuit between two fingers.
The poodle delicately took the biscuit in her teeth.

"More tea, Mr. Ratso?" Emily inquired, pouring
some cola from a can into the teacup. Ratso gave a
yawn, then leaned forward and lapped up the soda. He
gave a small burp, and Emily tsk-tsked with a shake
of her head. "We need to work on your table manners,
Mr. Ratso," she said. "But Miss Noelle is just divine."

Ginger grinned as she watched Jeannie smother her
laughter. They both looked up as Sam came toward
them from the barn, and Ginger groaned inwardly. He
looked like Wyatt Earp, out to clean up the town. If
the expression on his face was any indication, the tea
party was in trouble. She could picture Emily, Noelle
and Ratso behind bars, all three howling together.

"I'm training the dogs, Sam!" Emily called proudly
as he came closer.

Sam stopped by the table, a long-suffering look on
his face.

"Em, do you think you could teach that white hair-
ball to sleep at night?" he asked.

"I'm working on it, Sam," she assured him. "I'm

going to read her a bedtime story before I go home tonight."

"You do that, sweetheart." As he spoke, Ginger thought she saw a muscle twitch in his jaw. He gave Jeannie and Ginger a grim look before he went inside the house.

"Better face the music now," Jeannie said with a sigh. She and Ginger went inside just as Sam slammed his hat down on the counter. Jeannie started to tiptoe toward the front door, her fingers snagging her purse on the way. Ginger realized that she was the one who was going to face the music, and not Jeannie. Giving her an apologetic smile, Jeannie waved from the living room and quickly exited.

Sam turned when he heard the front door close.

"Going down with the ship alone?" he asked sarcastically. "It looks like your troops deserted you."

"I've got a kid and two guard dogs backing me up," she said, jerking her thumb toward the backyard. She sounded a lot cockier than she felt.

"Yeah, well, you might be interested to know that one of those guard dogs is hooked on soda. The kid turned my beagle into a Pepsi-head."

"I'm sure you can get him into a twelve-step program for beagles," she said. "And the kid will be gone soon." As soon as his mother left, she thought.

"Yeah, I suppose so," he said, his scowl deepening. He paused, then added, "Want to take the poodle with you when you go?"

Ginger grimaced wryly. "No way, cowboy. That there's your little dogie."

"It's doggie, not dogie," he said. "That poodle's no calf by any stretch of the imagination. More like an oversize Q-Tip. Hey,'' he said when Ginger started back to the stove. ''What say we call a truce here?''

''I don't recall starting hostilities,'' she said, jutting out her chin at him.

He was silent for a moment, and she thought that maybe he was just going to walk out. Then he shrugged.

''Okay.'' He sighed heavily. ''I see your point. Now, do you think maybe you could get Em to stop putting a hat on my beagle?''

''Maybe.''

''Maybe?'' He sounded incredulous.

''If I hear an apology.'' She stood her ground as he glared at her. She kept reminding herself that his bark was worse than his bite.

He looked as if he might start shouting at her instead, but she saw him control his temper with effort. He mumbled something and turned to leave.

''I beg your pardon?'' she said with exaggerated politeness.

''Sorry,'' he said. ''I shouldn't have started yelling at you for something that wasn't your fault.''

''That's more like it,'' she said, smiling for the first time.

''May I be excused now, ma'am?'' he asked dryly.

Ginger's smile widened. ''School's out for now, cowboy.''

Enid came downstairs just before dinnertime and set the table for Ginger. She kept eyeing her future daughter-in-law throughout the process, but Ginger was determined not to ask questions. Finally Enid gave a sigh.

''Sam was in a terrible mood this morning,'' she said. ''Jeannie said it was because Noelle howled all night, but I think it was something different.''

"Oh?" Ginger said noncommittally. "Did Noelle keep everyone awake?"

"Yes, she did," Enid said, narrowing her eyes as she surveyed Ginger. "And don't change the subject. We were talking about Sam's mood. He nearly bit off Jeannie's head this morning. And I heard him tell Ratso that if he wanted a Pepsi he'd have to learn to open the refrigerator door himself." She raised her brows. "I've *never* heard Sam yell at Ratso."

"He was just tired," Ginger said carefully as she cut shortening into the flour.

Enid snorted. "I've seen him tired before. And irritable. But something else is going on now. If I didn't know any better, I'd swear that my son was falling in love. But of course that can't be right, because he's already in love. Right?"

Ginger didn't dare look at Enid. She cleared her throat. "Right," she said without conviction. But she knew it wasn't true. Sam would never fall in love with her. He was too wary about women in general. And he had gone into this pretend engagement with his eyes wide open. He was the one who just last night had told her not to get any ideas about a real wedding. So Enid was way off the mark.

Enid started to say something else, but then she fell silent as the door opened and Sam walked in, with Emily and the dogs trailing behind him. Ratso no longer wore a hat, but the bow tie was still attached to his collar.

"And they'll both sit on command now," she was telling Sam. "But Ratso won't get up after he sits. Well, not unless I bribe him with Pepsi."

Sam gave Ginger a look that so much as said, *This*

is all your fault. He dragged off his hat and set it on the counter.

"Em," he said cautiously, "do you think it's a good idea to let that poodle in the house, with her...bad habits?"

"Oh, I taught her just to chew on her toys, Sam," Emily said earnestly.

"In just one day?"

"She's a good pupil," Emily told him. "She can already roll over. Watch." Emily called the poodle to her and held a dog biscuit in her hand. "Roll over, Noelle," she said. "Roll over, girl."

The poodle cocked her head and speculatively eyed the hand that held the biscuit. She danced a little on her feet, then sat back down as Emily repeated the command. Finally, she flopped over on her back and lay there, completely still.

Enid laughed. "I think Ratso taught her that one."

Ginger popped the biscuits she'd made into the oven, and fifteen minutes later they all sat down to dinner. She was aware of Sam's eyes on her while they ate, but she carefully avoided looking at him. If he was a man in love, he was doing a pretty good job of hiding it. In fact, he was doing just the opposite of what a man in love would do. Every other night he had held her chair and Enid's as they sat down for dinner, but tonight he helped Enid, then took his own seat. Enid's eyes went from one of them to the other, and then, to Ginger's surprise, she smiled.

Ginger frowned. Either Sam was letting her know, not so subtly, that she was on his Ten Least Wanted list, or else...

Or else the man was struggling against growing feelings for her. It made sense. And the fact that Enid seemed to find his reaction amusing lent credence to the theory. Ginger dared a look across the table at Sam and caught him watching her. He immediately looked down, and Ginger felt a surge of hope.

Sam helped her clean up after dinner, and her heart leaped when he told her to meet him outside when she was done.

Dusk was falling when she slipped out the back door, but the sky was darkening earlier than usual. She stood on the back porch a moment to look at the heavy clouds moving in from the west, then walked toward Sam, who was leaning against his pickup truck.

"Ready to ride?" he asked.

"Sure," Ginger said, trying to sound nonchalant. She moved toward the passenger side.

"We're not taking the truck," he said, a thread of amusement in his voice. She looked past him and for the first time noticed the horses saddled near the fence.

"I...don't know," she said, suddenly hesitant.

"What's the matter?" he teased her, a smile tugging up the corners of her mouth. "You still think Fire-cracker's going to buck you off into the nearest rose-bush?"

Ginger shook her head. Firecracker, she had discovered, was a softy. It was Sam Weller who worried her. If anyone was going to dump her into the nearest pile of thorns, it was this man. And it was all the worse because he knew how she felt about him.

Ginger tilted up her chin. "All right," she said coolly. "Let's ride."

The horses were edgy with the approaching storm, but Sam kept them under control easily. He led the way through the pasture without speaking. As the wind picked up, Ginger's hair whipped across her face, and she wished she'd thought to tie it back. With the growing darkness and a screen of hair impairing her vision, she had no idea where they were going.

When he finally stopped, she pushed her hair back and stared. They were on the opposite side of the lake, near the dock. She frowned and looked around, still holding her hair back. Firecracker shifted beneath her and snorted softly. Small whitecaps whipped up on the lake like dollops of soft cream. They lapped at the dock, barely visible now in the waning light.

The dock.

Ginger made a small sound, part pleasure and part surprise. Sam had rebuilt the dock, and now it stretched cleanly over the water. She turned to face him.

"It looks terrific," she said, beginning to smile, then stopping when she saw how serious he was.

"I didn't do it just for you," he said immediately, and, despite the fact that she'd expected him to say something like that, she felt disappointment gather in her stomach.

"Of course you didn't," she said glibly. "If it had been for me, you would have built a gazebo, as well."

"Ginger, I don't want to hurt you. I know how you feel, and I can't give you what you want."

"I don't expect anything from you, Sam," she said, hoping her voice wasn't shaking. "Except for my paycheck."

Sam didn't say anything for a moment, while he studied her face. "You know," he said carefully, "you make me feel guilty."

"It's not me," she retorted. "It's the ranch that's making you feel guilty. You built that dock because you finally saw what this place is, what it should be.

It's not a run-down ranch, Sam. It was never that. This place is a home.''

"It was a hell for Denise," he snapped, refusing to meet her eyes. "And for my mother."

"*They* made it their *own* hell, Sam!" she said sharply, finally giving way to her anger at him for blaming himself. "Even your own mother knows that. You didn't turn Denise against you and the ranch. She did it to herself."

Sam stared at her for so long that she broke her gaze and frowned into the dark. She released her hair, and it whipped around her face again.

"And you think *you* could live here?" he asked, so quietly that she barely heard him above the wind.

"What does it matter what I think?" she demanded. "You've already made up your mind on that score." With that, she turned Firecracker and nudged her back toward the house.

There it was, she thought. The gunfight at high noon in front of the saloon. Only this one had been on a windy evening beside a beautiful dock. And she still didn't know who had shot whom. Maybe they were both wounded. All she understood was that if he kept blaming himself for other people's unhappiness, then they had no chance.

Sam refused to watch her go. He didn't turn his horse until the wind kicked up even more fiercely and the first heavy, cold raindrop fell. Then he followed her, pushing the horse until he caught up to her at the barn. Tersely he told her that he would take care of the horses and she should go inside.

Ginger gave him a long, speculative look, but she did as he said.

He got Firecracker unsaddled and bridled and turned

to his horse. Thunder rolled outside, and lightning lit the sky, sending a flash of illumination into the barn.

Hell, he thought. He'd been so caught up in what he was going to say to Ginger that he forgot about the cattle. He had noticed earlier that day that two of the heifers weren't with the rest of the herd. He suspected that they were somewhere in the back pasture, and he had better go try to find them. The back pasture, with its old trees and its rushing stream that threatened to flood with every rain, was no place for cattle in a storm.

But even the prospect of chasing down cattle couldn't erase Ginger's words from his head. She didn't know what she was saying, he told himself. She couldn't like this ranch, the isolation, the lack of city amenities. But his conviction on that count had been wavering for days now. And last night he had finally admitted to himself that Ginger wasn't like Denise. She wasn't like his mother, either. And that left him more unsettled than not.

He made a dash for the house, figuring he would grab a flashlight there and head back to the pasture. Rain was pouring from his hair when he came in the back door.

Ginger turned from the sink, where she had obviously been watching out the window. She didn't say anything, but he could see the questions in her eyes. And he didn't have any answers for her.

"I have to go back to the pasture," he said tersely. "Go on home as soon as the rain lets up."

"I'll wait," she said, quietly, but with a determined edge.

Sam shrugged. "Suit yourself." He pulled on his poncho and stuck a flashlight in his pocket. The next minute, he was gone again, pulling the hood of his poncho over his head as he ran for the barn. Ginger cupped her hands to her forehead and leaned against the window, trying to see through the rain. She thought she caught sight of Sam on horseback heading toward the pasture, but the wind was blowing the rain nearly sideways by now, and she couldn't be sure.

"It's getting bad out," Enid said behind her. "Did Sam come in yet?"

"No," Ginger said, still looking out the window. "He went to the pasture."

Enid sighed. "Those cows again."

Those cows were his livelihood, but Ginger didn't say that.

"Mom, are we going to spend the night here?" Emily asked. Ginger turned and saw her standing uncertainly in the doorway.

"No, honey. We'll leave after Sam comes back and the storm lets up."

"Okay. I'll read Noelle and Ratso their bedtime story."

Ginger smiled as Emily went back to the living room, then returned to her window vigil. After watching her a moment, Enid went back upstairs.

After half an hour, Ginger left the window and made some coffee. Another half hour later, Sam still hadn't returned. The lightning had intensified, and a couple of times she had heard a loud crack from the vicinity of the pasture. The lights flickered, and Ginger began to pace. Enid came back to the kitchen to rummage through the refrigerator.

She sighed as she pulled out a plate with one piece of chocolate cream pie on it.

"I know you were saving this for Sam," she said,

"but he's out there, I'm in here, and it's finders keepers." When Ginger didn't say anything, Enid said, "Don't worry about him, honey. He and his dad were always gallavanting around in the worst possible weather checking on those cows. It never seemed very productive to me. They could have just as easily taken a look at the hamburger in the freezer."

"I'm going to go look for him," Ginger said, as if she hadn't heard. She grabbed one of Sam's jackets from the hook by the back door and the spare set of truck keys from a kitchen drawer. "He might be lying in a ditch, with no way to get help."

Enid raised her brows skeptically, but she didn't say anything, only sighed and shook her head as Ginger dashed out the door, the wind slamming it shut behind her.

Immediately she wished she had tied something over her head. Her hair and face were drenched in the short run to the truck. Once inside, she tried to calm herself by thinking about the mechanics of getting the truck from the drive to the pasture.

She got the engine started, then carefully let the clutch out with the gears in reverse. Back up. Brake. Clutch back in. Shift to first.

She made it to the gate and climbed out long enough to open it. Then, of course, she had to get out again to close it after driving through it. Pushing the wet hair out of her eyes, she clenched the steering wheel and edged her way through the pasture. She could hardly see anything for the rain, and she swore softly. Several times she had to drive around huge downed tree limbs, and once a whole tree.

The ground was so soft from the pounding rain that she was afraid to stop the truck to call to Sam, because she might get stuck. She felt as if she had been driving forever when the headlights picked up a shape ahead. Ginger strained to see whether it was another large tree limb down or something else. It looked like a figure on the ground. She stopped the truck, then tried to go forward again, but she was stuck. Gritting her teeth in frustration, she threw open the truck door and jumped down, nearly swamping herself in mud.

She ran forward as Sam stood up. She gave a sigh of relief because he didn't look as if he were hurt.

"Are you all right?" she cried over the wind and rain.

"Turn off the truck lights before you run down the battery," he shouted back, and she could cheerfully have punched him. She had been so worried, and he couldn't think of anything but a battery.

"I was afraid you'd been hurt!" she said when she got back to him after turning out the lights. She could hardly keep her hands from checking him for injuries.

And he looked at her as if she had gone mad.

"Hell, you've got my truck stuck in the mud," he said in irritation, glancing with a frown toward the truck.

"Well, excuse me," she snapped. "But your safety seemed a little more important than your damn truck. I was worried that you'd been mugged or something."

"Mugged?" He seemed amused now. "Now, who would mug me out here? One of the cows?"

"I can only hope," she snapped. "And what was taking you so long, anyway?"

"I've got a heifer that got hit by a falling tree," he said. "But the vet's on the way. Everything's under control. Except for my truck," he added with a touch of irritation.

"The vet's on the way," she repeated stupidly. "How did you get the vet?"

"My cell phone," he told her, gesturing toward his pocket. "Hey, are you all right? You look a little..."

"Distraught?" she finished for him, her patience evaporating. She was soaked to the bone, her shoes had absorbed five pounds of mud, her pants were ruined, she was half beside herself with worry, and he was assuring her that everything was under control. And he'd had a cell phone with him all the time!

"You don't—" she sputtered. "You can't possibly—" But there were no words for the aggravation she felt. There was only the satisfaction she would get from killing him right this moment. No jury with even one woman on it would ever convict her.

"You were worried, weren't you?" he said, comprehension finally dawning. They both stood in the pouring rain, the wind lashing their hair, staring at each other.

And then Sam pulled her to him, flat up against his chest, and kissed her. He kissed her so hard that she felt as if the force of the storm had gathered itself into his mouth.

She was breathless and half-dizzy when he stopped, but her anger hadn't abated.

"Don't you dare try to appease me that way!" she cried.

"The truck's dry inside," he said in a low voice, his hands stroking her shoulders. "I could do a much better job of appeasing you in there, sweetheart."

"You...you...oversexed, ignorant...cowboy!" She spit out the words, giving him a shove for good measure. "It serves you right that Enid ate your chocolate cream pie!"

He swayed but stayed on his feet, and Ginger spun around and began stomping back toward the house.

"Wait in the truck!" Sam called after her. "You're already drenched!"

But she paid him no mind, picking her way through the mud with as much dignity as she could muster, unmindful of the rain that ran down her face and hair and under her clothes.

Sam watched her with a mixture of confusion and aggravation. What the hell had she been thinking about, to come out here looking for him? No one had ever been worried enough about him to set out in the middle of a rainstorm to see if he was all right. No one but Ginger.

He began to smile, and then the smile turned into a chuckle. Finally, he threw back his head and laughed, letting the rain wash his face.

It was another hour later by the time the vet left and Sam had the cow safely sheltered in the barn. He was dead tired, and as wet as if he'd gone swimming, but he was still smiling. He stepped into the kitchen and noticed for the first time how much more inviting it was with the curtains at the windows and that drawing of Emily's that Ginger had stuck on his refrigerator. The comforting smell of the stew still hung in the room. This was a home, he realized for the first time.

Enid padded into the kitchen in her robe and slippers and yawned.

"Got those little cows all tucked in for the night?" she asked.

"Where's Ginger?"

"She took Emily home about an hour ago. Oh, and I'm sorry I ate your pie. Something came over me."

Sam pulled the milk from the refrigerator and smiled at her. "Join the club, Mother. I think something just came over me too."

He took a long swallow from the carton, and Enid clucked her tongue.

"Ginger's going to have your butt for that," she warned him.

"I know," he said, and he started grinning all over again.

Enid shook her head. She didn't know what was going on in Sam's head, but she didn't think any of her herbal concoctions were going to do the trick this time.

12

Sam couldn't believe that Ginger was still mad at him.

It was Friday, and she hadn't said more than two words at a time to him since the night of the storm. Unfortunately, those words usually were *Go away.*

He had tried to talk to her several times since then, but to his growing frustration, his mother was never far from either of them. He had tried calling Jeannie yesterday, ready to bribe her, if necessary, to spirit their mother away, just for an evening. Jeannie had suggested that the price was another poodle, this one the littermate of Noelle. Remembering two chewed rugs, a stain on the living room floor and continuous howling, Sam had hung up on his sister.

Now he listened with barely contained irritation as his mother chatted on the phone with Mary Stafford, inviting her to a dinner that night to celebrate Sam's engagement.

Enid hung up and made a pencil mark beside Mary's name on the list she was consulting.

"What did you do, invite the entire city?" he demanded.

"No, dear, just some close friends. Mary and that nice Mrs. Turner from the fudge shop, and of course Jeannie and Pete, and the sweet little dear who gave you Noelle, and the woman from the bridal shop, and—"

"Stop!" Sam burst out. "It sounds more like a wedding than a dinner."

Ginger came into the kitchen carrying a load of sheets for the laundry and eyed them both suspiciously. "What sounds more like a wedding?" she asked.

"Oh, just a little dinner party I'm planning for tonight," Enid said brightly. "I wanted to celebrate your engagement before I leave for home Sunday. I thought we could reserve a room at that nice restaurant on the river. I've been calling some friends."

"She's been calling half the phone book," Sam groused.

"Oh, no," Ginger said, setting down the basket. "Not a dinner party."

"Why, what's wrong, dear?" Enid asked.

Ginger cringed inwardly. There was no way she was going to smile for a whole roomful of people in a restaurant, when she was feeling so miserable.

She had made a royal fool of herself with Sam during the storm, and she couldn't face the additional embarrassment of pretending he was in love with her any longer. There was no way she was going to get trapped in a restaurant, smiling and accepting congratulations from people who thought Sam was going to marry her.

"I hate to disappoint you, Enid," Ginger said gently, "but I imagine the restaurant's booked up on Friday night."

"Oh, don't worry about it, dear," Enid assured her. "We can move the party here. Won't that be fun?"

It would be anything but fun. Unfortunately, there didn't seem to be a choice. Enid was already dialing another number, and Ginger refused to ask Sam for help.

"Mother—" Sam began in exasperation, then apparently gave up the fight. "All right. Have it your way, Mother. We'll have a party. I'll do some barbecue."

"Oh, that's lovely!" Enid said. "And, Ginger, do you think you could run me into town to get some things at the deli? I already picked up a cake at the bakery." Enid began to talk to whoever had answered the phone on the other end, inviting them to a barbecue at the ranch that evening, and Ginger sighed. Obviously, Enid was having a party, whether the two guests of honor wanted one or not.

She glanced at the clock. It was a little after one now. She could run Enid into town when she picked up Emily from school. With any luck, they would have food ready when Enid's guests came calling that evening.

The guests began arriving at six, and Ginger noted that, miraculously, it looked as though the party had been in the works for weeks. Sam had hung plastic party lights in the trees, and Ginger had put red plastic covers on the two picnic tables he'd resurrected from the barn. She had mixed up a big pitcher of margaritas while Enid got out some wineglasses and rolled the rims in lemon juice, then salt. Sam was barbecuing hamburgers on a grill outside, while Noelle and Ratso looked on longingly.

The only thing missing was some genuine affection between the couple whose engagement was being celebrated. Unfortunately, that wasn't something that Ginger could pick up at the deli. She glanced over at Sam as she carried a tray of margaritas to the tables and saw him watching her, an unreadable expression on his face. She knew that he had been trying hard to get her alone ever since the storm, but she had been working hard at avoiding him. She knew what he wanted—he'd make another apology, and then she would say, *Everything's fine, Sam, don't worry about it*. Only everything wasn't fine, and she couldn't pretend it was any longer.

She had fallen in love with Sam, but he continued to torture both of them with his idiotic belief that he and the ranch would drive her away. He was the stubbornest cowboy she'd ever met, and one day she would tell him that—if she ever saw him again after his mother went home on Sunday. Just thinking about that made her sad, and she marched herself back into the kitchen to keep her mind off Sam and her troubles with him.

Sam watched her go, his frown still firmly in place. He had decided that he would put a stop to her aggravating avoidance of him the instant this party was over. He had some things to tell her, and she was going to listen, if he had to tie her up to keep her in one place while he talked. She was the most independent, irritating woman he had ever met, and he didn't think he could survive without her.

The problem was, he didn't know how to tell her that. He had never felt this frustrated before in his life. But he was damn well going to tell her *something* before the night was over.

"I don't think that burger's going to talk, no matter how hard you lean on it," a voice at his elbow advised him. Sam glanced up to see Mary Stafford eyeing him with amusement, then down to note that he had pressed one hamburger nearly flat with his spatula. He quickly tried to pry it up, but it was stuck to the grill.

"Rough day?" Mary asked sympathetically.

"Rough two weeks," he admitted grudgingly.

Mary laughed. "Enid can try one's patience now and then."

"Not Mother," he admitted. "*That* woman in there." He gestured toward the kitchen with his shoulder.

Mary's brows went up. "Your fiancée?"

"The very same."

"So." Mary grinned. "She got to you, didn't she?"

Sam gave her a dark look. "No, she didn't get to me," he said. "She's just…aggravating."

Mary gave a satisfied chuckle. "She got to you."

She strolled away with her margarita, and Sam sighed. He felt as if the evening would never end.

But the evening finally did grind to a slow stop. It was about nine when the guests began drifting home. Emily had fallen asleep on the couch, Noelle and Ratso curled up at her feet. Emily's tiny bowed mouth was slack, and her lashes were dark against her cheek. Both dogs were snoring.

Ginger smiled as she tucked an afghan around Emily's shoulders. Her little girl had loved the party, going from one person to the next all evening, carrying her Kool-Aid and commanding Noelle and Ratso to heel. Of course, they hadn't. Most of the time, they flopped on the ground and promptly fell asleep. Ginger was beginning to think that Enid had a point. Maybe both canines had narcolepsy.

She jumped when she felt a hand on her shoulder. She spun around to see Sam studying her.

"They were certainly wound up tonight," he said softly, nodding toward the couch.

Ginger stood stiffly in front of him. "Wound up hardly describes two dogs who spend most of their life sleeping," she said dryly.

"They walked at least ten feet tonight," Sam said. "That's aerobic exercise for Ratso."

Ginger couldn't summon up a smile. She was too drained from her efforts to keep Sam at a distance. This was so much harder than she'd thought it would be. This past week had felt like a lifetime.

"I want to talk to you," Sam said. "Let's take a walk."

"I'm a little tired tonight," she said, not looking at him. "Maybe tomorrow."

Sam's jaw tightened. "You're not getting out of this. We'll have our talk right here and now."

Ginger tried to think of some excuse to leave the room and put some distance between them, but she didn't have to worry. Jeannie came breezing into the room through the front door, a stack of dishes in her hands.

"Don't mind me," she called gaily. "Just thought I'd pick up the stuff on the porch. "Looks like everybody had a good time." She glanced from Sam to Ginger, a puzzled look crossing her face. "I'll just—"

"Never mind," Sam said sharply. "Come on," he said to Ginger, taking her hand and pulling her toward the kitchen. If she didn't want to put up a fuss in front of Jeannie, she had no choice but to follow. Sam slowed only momentarily, but when he saw Pete at the sink, loading the dishwasher, he dragged Ginger through the back door and into the shadows under the eaves.

Ginger snatched her hand away from him the moment they were alone. "If you're through manhandling me now, I should be going," she snapped.

"You're not going anywhere until I have my say," Sam said, leaning one hand against the house on either side of her shoulders so that she was trapped. "I've been trying to talk to you for days, and you keep giving me the slip."

"Maybe because I know what you're going to say," she shot back, glaring at him challengingly.

"And what is that?"

"That you're sorry about what you said, but commitment isn't in your future and couldn't we just be friends?" She jutted out her chin, facing him defiantly.

It was so close to the truth that he was momentarily taken aback. It was what he would like to say, all right, but somehow he couldn't seem to make himself believe the words anymore.

"I do want us to be friends," he said finally, and realized from the way she tightened her mouth that he was only confirming her worst suspicions. "And more," he added tersely.

She waited two heartbeats, then asked, "What do you mean by more?"

"I want to see you after my mother's gone home," he said. "On a personal basis."

"Meaning?"

Sam made a growling sound deep in his throat. "You're making this hard for me, you know that, sweetheart?"

"You're damn right," she snapped back, as ready to do battle as he was. "Are we talking a paycheck kind of thing here, or what?"

"Jeez, no," he muttered. "I thought maybe we

could…date.'' There. He'd said it. He'd gotten that vile word past his throat. He felt as if he'd just asked her to go to a pornographic movie with him, and from the expression on her face, she felt the same way.

''Are you sure you don't want to write a check for that, too?'' she asked, baiting him. ''That's your style, isn't it? Pay any sum as long as it protects you from permanent commitment.''

''Hey,'' Sam said, not at all sure he liked the turn this discussion was taking. ''As I recall, you didn't voice any big objections to taking that paycheck for services rendered. And now that I'm willing to continue things without any monetary considerations, you're backpedaling like a canoeist approaching Niagara Falls.''

''So what are you saying?'' she countered. ''That you want to date me with no strings attached?''

''Yeah,'' Sam said, getting a bit riled. ''Isn't that what I said? Date and…stuff.''

''What kind of stuff?''

''Damn, you sure want a lot of details here.''

''What kind of stuff?'' Ginger repeated stubbornly. ''You mean sleep together, don't you?''

''Well, yeah, that, too.'' At least Sam had the grace to look uncomfortable. Ginger supposed it was a point in his favor that he realized what a jerk he was being on that point.

''No strings, no paycheck, no commitment, just…*dating*,'' Ginger said, making the word sound like *prostituting*.

Sam knew when he was beat, but he wasn't about to give up the fight, at least not without one last try.

''Okay,'' he said, removing his hands and shoving them into his pockets. ''What if we were engaged?''

"We *are* engaged," she retorted.

"I mean for real," he said from between gritted teeth. "The ring stays on your hand. I'm not saying we'd set a real date. But it would definitely be an engagement."

"Sam Weller," she said, "are you asking me to marry you?"

"I guess so," he said, sounding more like a man confessing to a crime than one who had just proposed marriage.

"I'll think about it," she said loftily.

"You'll *what?*" Sam demanded, his temper barely held in check. "Well, think about this," he said, and before Ginger could move, his head dipped to hers and he kissed her, long, slow and hard.

Oh, my.

She always had that reaction to his kisses, as if he had just made love to her with heart and soul. The man drove her crazy, with words and with his touch. And now he was proposing—well, sort of proposing.

"I...think..." she murmured when he finally lifted his head. "I mean...uh...okay."

"Okay what, sweetheart? You aren't overthinking this, are you?"

Ginger shook her head. "No. I mean, I accept."

Sam began to smile, and he leaned down to kiss her again, softly this time, and with a sensual need.

Ginger was lost, and only dimly aware that someone had begun to applaud. Even after Sam raised his head and looked around, she didn't quite grasp what was happening.

"Ha! I knew this would work!"

Enid stood just to their side, near the door, a big grin on her face. The screen door was open, and Jeannie stood there uncomfortably shifting her weight from one foot to the other, shooting her mother worried glances.

"Maybe I ought to fix you some coffee, Mother," Jeannie said, trying to take her mother by the arm. "I think you might be one margarita over your limit."

"Nonsense," Enid said, resisting the pressure on her arm. "Besides, you and I have reason to celebrate tonight. It's not every day that I get my stubborn son to do something I want him to do." She grinned, swaying a bit on her feet.

"What are you saying?" Sam demanded, and Ginger saw the warning look in his eyes, even if Enid did not.

Enid planted her hands on her hips. "I'm saying that Jeannie and I snookered you, my dear son. My visit—and your sudden, desperate need of a fiancée—were cooked up by Jeannie and me. Didn't think your old mother had it in her, did you? And the best part is, it worked. You and Ginger didn't have much going for the two of you as a couple, other than a little chemistry, when I got here. Any idiot could have seen that. But now..." She beamed in triumph. "Now, I'd say you're on the path to the altar for real."

"Congratulations, Mother," Sam said coldly, and Ginger shivered at his tone. His eyes cut to her, and she would have stepped backward at the coldness there if she wasn't already up against the wall. "Nice plan you had there," he said, almost offhandedly. "You played your part to perfection. Too bad I found out before you actually got me to the altar."

"I didn't..." she began, but she knew it was useless. He wanted to believe that she was part of this plot to marry him off, and he would believe it no matter what she said.

"Sam, wait," Jeannie said, but he had already spun on his heel and was stalking toward the barn. "Oh, this is just great," Jeannie muttered, giving her mother an accusing look. Then she looked at Ginger and softened. "I'm sorry, Ginger," she said.

But Ginger was afraid that she might fall apart right then and there if she allowed herself to accept any sympathy. She had to get out of there right this minute.

"I have to go home," she said, hurrying past Jeannie into the kitchen. She grabbed her purse, called Emily's name to wake her, and tried to find her jacket through a blur of tears. Jeannie came into the kitchen and said her name softly, but Ginger pretended not to hear. A moment later she was hurrying to her car, all but carrying a half-asleep Emily.

The hardest part was explaining to Emily why they weren't going to go to the ranch anymore. The second hardest was returning the engagement ring to Mary Stafford and hurrying away before she asked questions.

It was a week since Enid's inebriated confession had made Sam walk away from her. She hadn't heard a word from him. Enid had made Jeannie stop at Ginger's shop on their way to the airport the previous Sunday, and she had given Ginger the check that Sam had written for her.

"I'm sorry," Enid said, patting Ginger's hand. "I shouldn't have meddled." She sighed. "But you're so right for Sam. Jeannie phoned me right after she met you and told me about you. When Jeannie's attempts to get the two of you together didn't work, we cooked up my visit to get him moving."

"Well, it was a nice thought," Ginger said, trying

to smile and trying to believe that no harm had been done.

"But look what he ended up with instead of you," Jeannie protested. "A French poodle who eats socks."

"She's been eating socks?" Ginger asked.

"Four so far. And none of them match." She gave a sigh much like Enid's. "And the strangest part is that Sam isn't even upset with her. He doesn't raise his voice at anything or anyone, not even me. He hasn't been sleeping well, and it's not because of Noelle's howling." Jeannie met Ginger's eyes, then looked away. "He didn't answer the phone one morning, so Pete and I went out to check on him. He *always* has the cell phone with him. We found him coming in from the back pasture. He said he'd gotten up at three because he couldn't sleep. He said he *likes* riding out and checking on the cattle at three in the morning. He never was a very good liar."

"I'm sorry," Ginger said, feeling her heart wrench with pain. It didn't ease her misery any to know that Sam was suffering, as well. They would both get over it, she told herself.

But, if anything, her misery was becoming more unbearable as the week wore on. Today was Saturday, her jobs were all completed, and she had a whole empty day stretching out before her. And she couldn't think of a darn thing she wanted to do.

But she had to do something. She couldn't sit around the shop and wonder what Sam was doing, whether he was missing her. Of course he wasn't missing her. He'd paid her off, and now he probably thought he was well rid of her.

Ginger pulled herself together and decided to take

Emily shopping. That was always good for wiping an irritating man out of a woman's memory bank.

The shopping actually helped relax her a bit, and though the ice cream cone she and Emily got on the way home reminded her a lot of Sam's penchant for ice cream, she was feeling a lot better when she turned up their street. The sun was setting, and she felt almost peaceful. Mrs. Turner's granddaughter was sitting in front of the fudge shop, and Emily begged to be allowed to play with her.

Ginger parked in front of the fudge shop, and after checking with Mrs. Turner and instructing Emily to stay there until she came back for her later, Ginger gathered her packages and walked toward her own shop.

Her footsteps slowed, and any small sense of peace deserted her. Lounging against her doorway was Sam Weller, his cowboy hat drawn low over his eyes so that she couldn't read his expression.

Her mouth went dry at the sight of the tight jeans encasing those long, muscular legs and the soft blue chambray shirt rolled up to his elbows. But her heart's pounding was more than erotic memory when she saw the tight line of his mouth. She was suddenly wary. What did he want now?

Ginger refused to meet his eyes as she drew even with him. He waited a moment, then stepped aside so that she could unlock her door. He followed her inside, still without saying anything, and she put down the packages, realizing that her hands were shaking.

"You didn't cash the check," he said at last, and she turned slowly to face him.

"I don't want your money," she said, trying to keep her voice even. Her heart sank. Was money what this was about? "I don't want anything from you," she said defiantly.

"I can think of one thing you might want," he said cryptically, and she flushed. "Come with me, and I'll show you."

Ginger shook her head. "I don't think so."

"What's the matter, sweetheart? Are you afraid of what I might do? I still haven't paid you back for miring my truck in mud, you know."

"I'm not afraid of you," she snapped, but it wasn't true. She knew that he would never hurt her physically, but her heart couldn't take any more of his rejection. She was as emotionally vulnerable as she'd been the last time she saw him.

"Then come with me," he said challengingly.

Ginger crossed her arms over her chest. "And if I do—will you leave me alone after that?"

He inhaled sharply, and she saw what looked like grim fear in his eyes. "It's a deal. You want to call it quits after this, then...okay."

"Let's go, then." She started for the door, feeling him following behind her.

She wouldn't speak on the drive to the ranch, and she wouldn't look at him. Sam could feel his nerves bunched in knots in his chest. Maybe this hadn't been a good idea after all. He knew she was hurt, but he hadn't expected this cold, uninterested tightness in her. Maybe she didn't love him after all. That thought hit him like a kick in the stomach. But he'd come too far now to let that stop him.

When they got to the ranch, he stopped the truck and turned to face her.

"This next part requires a little patience on your part."

Her brows went up immediately. ''I think I've been more than patient, considering the job you hired me to do. Playing your fiancée took a *lot* of patience.''

Sam sighed. ''Please.'' He pulled a clean bandanna from his pocket and reached out to her.

''What are you doing?'' she demanded, jerking away.

''Blindfolding you.''

''*What?* Are you crazy?''

''For someone who was engaged to me, you sure seem to ask that question a lot.'' He frowned.

''I ask it a lot because I have serious doubts about your sanity,'' she said, regarding him darkly. ''Why do you even think I would let you blindfold me?''

''Because you love me,'' he said without hesitation, and Ginger turned away from him.

''You won't be sorry,'' he said softly, slipping the cloth over her eyes and tying it gently in back.

''Too late,'' she whispered hoarsely. ''I'm already sorry.''

He didn't say anything, but his big, callused hand stroked her neck softly. ''Don't be,'' he murmured.

Then he started the truck. He stopped once and got out, then got in again, moved a bit and got back out. She realized that they must be heading for the pasture and he was opening and closing the gate. The truck bumped over the ruts left by the storm, and she clutched the seat to keep from being jarred off it. She didn't know what he could possibly show her that would make any difference in their relationship, but she had gone this far.

The truck finally stopped, and he got out. He opened her door and put his arms around her waist, holding her against him as he helped her out of the truck. She reached for the blindfold, but his hand covered hers.

"Not yet," he said quietly.

He helped her navigate the rough terrain with his hands on her shoulders, but suddenly he scooped her up in his arms.

"What are you doing?" she demanded.

"Jeez, but you're an impatient woman," he complained. "Just one more little minute."

She bit back her irritated retort and waited. She heard something hollow echo under his feet, but she still hadn't figured out where they were. He set her down and turned her until he was satisfied.

Slowly and carefully, he removed her blindfold.

Ginger blinked and pushed back her hair. It was almost twilight, but she could see the last reflections of the setting sun on water.

The dock. She was standing on the dock. Only there was a roof over her head. She turned in place, taking in the new wood, the benches built into the walls, the arched dome above. She tilted her head up and gasped.

There it was. Her stained-glass window. Three of them, in fact. They steepled together in a peak that capped the roof. The last light from the sun glinted through them, sending sprays of red and green and blue across the wooden floor.

Here was the grand gesture she'd always wanted.

"My stained glass!" she cried. "You put in my gazebo."

"And a hell of a job it was, sweetheart," he told her. "That's what took a whole week. I couldn't find anyone who could put together a stained-glass window in a couple of days, so I did it myself."

"*You* did this for me?" she asked in wonder. "But,

you said it's so…impractical. You said the mosquitoes would eat me alive.''

''Oh, they will,'' he assured her. ''But you'll be sitting in your very own gazebo, looking up at your very own stained-glass window, while they dine on you. But I should warn you—I'm going to be nibbling on you, too. I didn't build this thing to let you sit out here all alone.'' He raised his brows. ''You see how wide that bench is? I measured it. Not quite as big as a bed, but it'll do. Of course, you might need to put a nice soft cushion on it for comfort.''

''What are you saying?'' she asked, feeling tears gather in her eyes.

''I'm saying that I love you. I want a long-term contract on that rent-a-wife deal. I'm saying I don't think I got my money's worth the first time.''

''And when do you think you'll have your money's worth?'' she asked softly, dying to touch him.

''Oh, I figure in about fifty or sixty years. We can renegotiate then. What do you say?''

''I want to see your eyes,'' she said, trying to look into his face.

Slowly, Sam took off his cowboy hat, and Ginger saw the emotion in his face, the love in his eyes, the same longing she felt in her heart. It was all there, everything she'd wanted.

Sam fell silent, worried because she wasn't saying anything. ''You aren't backing out now, are you?'' he asked, his voice uneven.

''Aren't you afraid I'll get tired of the ranch?'' she asked. ''Tired of you?''

So that was what was worrying her. Him and his stupid anxieties about bringing a woman here. He began to smile.

"Naw, never entered my mind," he said, deciding to tease her again. "You see, honey, you're one of those women who's easily amused. And what with two dogs and several kids—"

"*Several kids?*" she repeated, her eyes widening.

"See, that's how I figure I'll keep you happy here on the ranch. Between me and the dogs and the kids and your business, you won't have time to get bored."

"Oh, there's one other thing I'm going to spend a lot of time thinking about," she assured him, beginning to smile herself. "You see, there's this big, handsome cowboy, a bit stubborn at times, and I'm going to find all kinds of reasons to get him into bed with me."

Sam's grin widened. "This is going to be real interesting," he said, just before he crushed her to him for a deep kiss that made Ginger's toes curl.

Oh, my.

* * * * *

THE BABY OF THE MONTH CLUB

RITA-Award-Winning Author

MARIE FERRARELLA's

*miniseries continues with her
brand-new Silhouette single title*

In The Family Way

Dr. Rafe Saldana was Bedford's most popular pediatrician. And though the handsome doctor had a whole lot of love for his tiny patients, his heart wasn't open for business with women. At least, not until single mother Dana Morrow walked into his life. But Dana was about to become the newest member of the Baby of the Month Club. Was the dashing doctor ready to play daddy to her baby-to-be?

Available June 1998.

Silhouette®

Find this new title by Marie Ferrarella
at your favorite retail outlet.

Take 4 bestselling love stories FREE

Plus get a FREE surprise gift!

Special Limited-time Offer

Mail to Silhouette Reader Service™

3010 Walden Avenue
P.O. Box 1867
Buffalo, N.Y. 14269-1867

YES! Please send me 4 free Silhouette Yours Truly™ novels and my free surprise gift. Then send me 4 brand-new novels every other month, which I will receive months before they appear in bookstores. Bill me at the low price of $2.90 each plus 25¢ delivery and applicable sales tax, if any.* That's the complete price and a savings of over 10% off the cover prices—quite a bargain! I understand that accepting the books and gift places me under no obligation ever to buy any books. I can always return a shipment and cancel at any time. Even if I never buy another book from Silhouette, the 4 free books and the surprise gift are mine to keep forever.

201 SEN CF2X

Name	(PLEASE PRINT)	
Address		Apt. No.
City	State	Zip

This offer is limited to one order per household and not valid to present Silhouette Yours Truly™ subscribers. *Terms and prices are subject to change without notice. Sales tax applicable in N.Y.

USYRT-296

BEVERLY BARTON

**Continues the
twelve-book series—
36 Hours—in April 1998
with Book Ten**

NINE MONTHS

Paige Summers couldn't have been more shocked when she learned that the man with whom she had spent one passionate, stormy night was none other than her arrogant new boss! And just because he was the father of her unborn baby didn't give him the right to claim her as his wife. Especially when he wasn't offering the one thing she wanted: his heart.

For Jared and Paige and *all* the residents of Grand Springs, Colorado, the storm-induced blackout was just the beginning of 36 Hours that changed *everything!* You won't want to miss a single book.

Available at your favorite retail outlet.

Look us up on-line at: http://www.romance.net

SC36HRS10

Catch more great

HARLEQUIN™ Movies

featured on the movie channel tmc

Premiering April 11th
Hard to Forget
based on the novel by bestselling
Harlequin Superromance® author
Evelyn A. Crowe

Don't miss next month's movie!
Premiering May 9th
The Awakening
starring Cynthia Geary and David Beecroft
based on the novel by Patricia Coughlin

If you are not currently a subscriber to
The Movie Channel, simply call your
local cable or satellite provider for more
details. Call today, and don't miss out
on the romance!

the movie channel tmc

100% pure movies.
100% pure fun.

HARLEQUIN™

Makes any time special.™